Lucas Malet

Mrs. Lorimer

Volume II

Lucas Malet

Mrs. Lorimer
Volume II

ISBN/EAN: 9783741123696

Manufactured in Europe, USA, Canada, Australia, Japa

Cover: Foto ©Andreas Hilbeck / pixelio.de

Manufactured and distributed by brebook publishing software
(www.brebook.com)

Lucas Malet

Mrs. Lorimer

MRS. LORIMER

A SKETCH IN BLACK AND WHITE

BY

LUCAS MALET

VOL. II.

London

MACMILLAN AND CO.

1883

MRS. LORIMER.

PART II.

CHAPTER I.

" A mere spectator of other men's fortunes and adven-
tures, and how they act their parts, which methinks
are diversely presented unto me, as from a common
theatre or scene. "

SOME people, I fear, may not unjustly
complain of the commonplace characters
and trivial incidents which they are in-
vited to contemplate in this little tale ;
and which are hardly worth the ink and
paper—let alone the time—that has been
wasted upon them. But I would protest,
with all humility and sincerity, that I do
not lay claim to the title of poet or
artist, still less to that of moralist or
preacher. Those who want illumination

and instruction must seek it elsewhere ;—
and surely in the present day it is easy
enough to get an immense amount of
information concerning all subjects at a
very small cost. Sometimes, indeed, one
is a little tempted to wonder whether the
teachers do not outnumber the scholars,
since most persons whom one meets with
are so willing to expound all dark sayings
and reveal all mysteries.

I have no claim to belong to the peda-
gogic and improving class ; and would
merely ask the gentle reader—if in these
enlightened days that kind and sympathetic being still exists—to picture some
lazy loiterer, arrayed in a torn cloak
and tattered jerkin, and a cap which
once had bells to it—their old-world
jangling was so sadly out of tune with the
triumphal war-march of modern progress,
that he pulled them all off long ago—
sitting among the dusty grass and wild
flowers, by the wayside of life, and telling

simple stories to the passers-by. Not
telling them to the wise and prudent
and successful, who would certainly call
him a sturdy beggar, a mere cumberer
of the ground, and bid him either set
about some useful business, or proceed to
improve himself off the face of the earth,
with all possible despatch : but telling
them to quiet ordinary folk, who are not
very wise or very successful, who are a
little confused with the turmoil and the
strife of tongues, and a little weary and
footsore with the journey ;—begging them
to rest awhile with him by the roadside,
and listen to simple tales of friendship
and of sorrow, of laughter and of lovers'
kisses ; begging them to judge gently all
the barren, groping, uncertain lives around
them, and to smile,—if they will,—but smile
very tenderly at the strange tragi-comedy of
every day. He has neither advice to give,
nor solution to offer—the poor Fool, in
his ragged motley, is hardly likely to have

discovered the panacea for this world's troubles, when the great and learned and courageous have failed so signally to do so. But he clings to one or two fantastic hopes that have lingered with us through many ages ; and does not despair, as he watches,—from amongst the dusty grass and flowers,—the anxious eager multitudes jostling each other along the great highroad, which stretches across the isthmus of this life, between the two eternities.

It is always an ungracious task to try to show any unvarnished side of truth ; and the unvarnished truth concerning themselves has usually been singularly unpalatable to members of the human family —only the Fool would attempt to present it. His acknowledged want of wits may save him from the angry punishments with which men are wont to visit the indiscretion of those who try to tell them what they really are. Under the shelter of the cap and bells, alone, can one venture to

say that absolute black and white, un-
doubted hero and villain, are hardly ever
to be met with ; and that heaven and hell
certainly belong to quite another state of
being than to this present one ;—that
original sin is pretty evenly distributed
among us all ;—that even the saint may
be caught wearing strangely dirty old
clothes, while the sinner is found arrayed,
now and then, in a garment of genuine
righteousness ;—that, while man is very
little higher than the beasts, he is, also,
very little lower than the angels.

In treating poor Elizabeth Lorimer's
character from this confusing and un-
satisfactory point of view, I know that
I run the risk of losing her many friends
and admirers. Yet, in truth, she was very
far from being an ideal woman. She
could neither satisfy those excellent persons who have a sentimental longing after
what has been called "the constant
mourner ;" nor could she please the more

light-minded class, who are disposed to recommend plenty of eating and drinking to-day, since the time for all such enjoyment may be passed and over by to-morrow. She was subtly compounded of good and evil, nobility and frivolity, of fine aspirations and commonplace selfishness. She was capable of determining against her higher instincts, and then repenting of her error, all too late, like many another young creature. She loved life, and would fain have seen good days ; and,—perhaps consequently,—she had but a misty and indistinct perception of the infinite value of a humble spirit and a broken and contrite heart.

Nearly a year had passed away since Elizabeth had made her compact with Fred Wharton in the quaintly-furnished studio down by the river. She had spent the early summer in London, and then had gone abroad with the Frank Lorimers,— Wharton, of course, being of the party,—

and had studied the art of Platonic friendship on the wild sea-shore and among the
bare windy uplands of Brittany. Her connection with Claybrooke had been re-
stricted to letters. She had offered to go
to the Rectory, it is true : but, unfortunately, she happened to propose herself just
at the time when Mr. and Mrs. Mainwaring
were about to make their yearly visit to
Selford ; and it was too much to expect
their dignified and stately plans to be set
aside for Elizabeth—whose appreciation of
Claybrooke and of its owners' society, her
aunt, at least, regarded as so distinctly
limited. Mr. Mainwaring had paid her one
or two visits in London, which were chiefly
remarkable for their extreme brevity. The
Rector, it must be confessed, did not find
himself in very active sympathy with his
niece's present surroundings.

Face downwards, in the narrow writing-
table drawer, still lay the charcoal sketch
of Robert Lorimer. Elizabeth had never

moved it from its resting-place since the day
when she had decided to forget the past,
and to try and find fresh joy and hope in
the future. In some fabrics it is possible
to patch a rent for a time ; but eventually the stuff gives and gives, and, as we
know, the new piece only makes the hole
in the old garment worse in the end.
Elizabeth's determination not to grieve for
her husband's death had, in a way, kept
her attention fixed on the fact of his
death. She had striven to patch the
cruel rent that had been made in her
happiness : but as time went on the
threads began to strain and give out, and
the sense of the magnitude of her misfortune grew greater, instead of lessening.

At moments, by the sea-shore, or on summer evenings when Fred Wharton poured
out his whole soul in music and in song, or
as she watched Frank and Fanny Lorimer
playing with their two children, the sense
of her own loss and loneliness would almost

overpower Elizabeth. She dreaded these feelings of sorrow, she fought against them, and was glad when the trivial interests of every day claimed her whole thought and attention. To her companions she seemed to be drifting farther and farther away from the past. She appeared gay and cheerful ; and yet there was an unrestfulness and a certain necessity for excitement about her, which puzzled Fanny Lorimer a little sometimes. She wondered whether Elizabeth was not developing feelings which could not, strictly, be described as Platonic for Fred Wharton.

But I think Elizabeth may be quite exonerated from any charge of this kind. She was almost painfully conscious that, if it were possible for her to meet Robert Lorimer now, for the first time, she might love him in a very different fashion, to that in which she had loved him when they met nearly three years before. As her experience of life widened and her knowledge of men and women increased, she appreciated more and more the true worth of her husband's character. She realised, too, how cruelly he must have suffered in bidding good-bye to life and love, in the very prime of his manhood. Elizabeth became aware that it might not be impossible for her to worship—all too late— the memory of the man whom she had loved very inadequately while he lived. That fashion of stoning the prophets, and subsequently—in a fit of bitter remorse— building them magnificent sepulchres, did not die out with the old dispensation : but is practised pretty freely by husbands and wives, parents and children, relations and friends, even to the present day.

If Fred Wharton had been asked to give a disquisition on Platonic friendship about this period, he would have pronounced it a very interesting, but slightly agitating, form of entertainment. He had seen a great deal of Elizabeth, he knew

her remarkably well; yet—carrying out his
old metaphor of the unexplored country—
he told himself that though the hills, and
valleys, and lakes, and streams, were very
delightful, there was still an unknown region, far inland, into which he had never yet
succeeded in penetrating. He was haunted
by the same notion as Fanny Lorimer—
namely, that some day Elizabeth would
develop suddenly, in an unlooked - for
direction, and surprise him very greatly.
There was something rather fascinating
in this idea; it made her all the more
interesting to him; yet it troubled him
too. Wharton hated surprises. He had
tried to imagine all sorts of combinations
of circumstances which might produce this
sudden development in Elizabeth, so that
he might be prepared for it when it came :
but he could not see his way at all
clearly yet. He told himself, however,
that women certainly were very interesting, and he began to neglect his other

friends a little. Men are comparatively easy
to understand ; they are nice comfortable
creatures : but make by no means such
suggestive and exciting companions, as a
handsome, brilliant, gray-eyed, young lady.

At the beginning of the winter season, that burning and shining light of
the dramatic profession, Clement Bartlett,
came out in a new piece. His friends
made a strong rally round him, filled
innumerable stalls, and applauded, even
his faintest efforts, with a vigour and
enthusiasm, which, it is to be feared, were
slightly incomprehensible to the rest of
the house. Be that as it may, on the
following day—a Sunday—Mr. Bartlett,
being anxious to thank his loyal supporters
and talk over the position with them generally, held a sort of levee in his rooms, in
the afternoon ; at which the members of
the " Modern Society of Friends "—as Mrs.
Frank called them—mustered in great
numbers. Frank Lorimer of course was

there. As the sub-editor and dramatic critic of a well-known paper, he was naturally very precious in the young actor's sight.

Fred Wharton went too,—not so much because he desired particularly to add his voice to the chorus of praise, as because he had nothing particular to do, and thought he should enjoy a walk across the park with Frank. He was rather silent and preoccupied. He had been working away at Platonic friendship for a long time now, and he found it more engrossing and bewildering than ever. He began to think a man wanted a very steady head who meant to go in for much of that sort of thing.

It was not till he and Frank were walking home under the bare black trees in the growing darkness, while the air was full of the sound of church-bells—that strange sound in which sorrow treads so hard on the heels of joy—calling faithful souls to their

evening prayers, that Wharton seemed with
a certain effort to shake off his preoccupa-
tion, and that he began to talk again.

" I'm rather dissatisfied with myself,
Frank," he remarked suddenly. " It is
a new sensation. I suppose it's a sign
that I am growing old."

Frank Lorimer was running over some
sentences in his mind, in which he was
trying to adjust the rival claims of friendship and truth in a critique on Clement
Bartlett's performance of the night before.
He answered at random, not thinking
what he was saying.

" Oh, you add dissatisfaction to all the
other disagreeables of old age then, do
you ?"

" I don't add it," answered Wharton
quickly. " Heaven preserve me from
adding one straw to a burden which I
shall have to bear myself some day ! It
will be quite heavy enough any way
without my private contributions. But

it is obvious," he added, "that old people must be dissatisfied with themselves.   If they have any powers of reflection left, they must be pretty keenly sensible of the immense number of mistakes they have succeeded in making in the course of their lives."

Frank Lorimer drew his hand down reflectively over his fair pointed beard. Really he could not honestly praise Clement Bartlett's performance very much. Fortunately there was the acknowledged excellence of the young man's figure to fall back upon : but it is rather difficult to fill half a column with a eulogy on a man's figure.   The public might object to it, and not without reason, Frank felt.   Meanwhile common civility demanded that he should make some comment on Wharton's dis-quisitions upon the distressing position of agèd and reflective souls.

"Are you painfully sensible of mistakes then, just now?" he asked abstractedly.

"I believe I am rather worried," answered the other.

This was such an entirely surprising announcement as coming from Fred Wharton, of all people in the world, that Frank Lorimer was roused effectually from his meditations upon Mr. Bartlett. He looked round sharply at his companion : but in the dusk it was difficult to catch the expression of his face.

"You're a little out of sorts, my dear fellow," said Frank. "You have taken to never going out anywhere. Half the men at Bartlett's this afternoon were complaining that they never see you now."

"It's a horrible thing," said Wharton, half laughing and half in earnest. "I am getting a little bored. I am beginning to feel uninterested."

"Oh, you are only hipped," answered the other. "You want more society."

"Perhaps I do," said Wharton uneasily. "I seem to be changing somehow ; I don't know quite what is coming over me. I used to look on at life so contentedly. I used to feel—I suppose all the talk at Clement Bartlett's this afternoon has put the idea into my head—as if I had got a very good private box at the general show. I just sat still and watched the play. I wasn't unsympathetic; indeed, sometimes I was inclined to applaud quite vigorously, and the tragic scenes upset me dreadfully. But I had a comfortable feeling that as I had not written the piece I was in no way implicated in the course of it. Now I begin to wonder whether I have not been rather cold-blooded, and whether I have not made a mistake in not being more actively human."

" Marry," observed Frank Lorimer, smiling. " It is the best cure for your state of mind. A wife is pretty sure to make you sufficiently human."

Wharton stopped, and said almost petulantly :—

" Why do you say that ?   It is tiresome.
It is dreadfully wanting in originality."

Frank was silent.   He did not understand his friend's sudden outburst of irrita-
bility.   He had spoken quite innocently,
and without any real desire that his advice
should be taken.   If he had been asked,
indeed, Frank would certainly have given
it as his opinion that Wharton would
probably never marry, that it would be
a pity if he should do so, as it would rob
him of half his present charm.

They walked on in silence for a little
while under the bare trees.   If people
were cross, Frank thought, it was always
safest to let them alone.   Bad temper
is like a cold in the head—it is much
best to let it have its course, instead
of rushing in with consolatory camphor,
and sal-volatile, and other well-intentioned
remedies, which generally end by merely
adding one or two new discomforts to the
original one.   Frank did not agitate him-

self, but relapsed into his difficult piece of criticism again.

"And I'm not at all sure that I am so very anxious to be cured of my present state of mind, after all," said Wharton after a pause. "Any way, I am not the least inclined to take the desperate measure you propose. The cure would be considerably more confusing than the disease, it seems to me. I am only angry with myself for feeling these things at all."

Frank had just got hold of an admirable sentence.

"Then don't feel them, my dear fellow," he said.

"I couldn't give up my attitude of spectator altogether, you know," Wharton went on argumentatively. He seemed to attach very much more importance to Frank Lorimer's random suggestion than it at all deserved. "Women are so differently constituted to us, that it is a thousand to one if I should find any woman—a

really charming one, you know—who
would be willing just to sit still and observe with me. She would get excited
some day, and want to go down on to the
stage into the thick of it all."

He paused, and then added lightly :—

" I am very philosophic, personally I am
not at all impulsive: but if she went down,
I am dreadfully afraid I should not have
sufficient strength of mind to let her go
alone."

" Probably not," answered Frank Lorimer, smiling.

" And that would be intolerable," said
Wharton. " It would upset all my system.
It would be the greatest mistake of all.
No," he added, as they passed out of the
comparative quiet of the Park into the
noise and movement of Piccadilly ; " marriage is out of the question from my point
of view."

CHAPTER II.

" When all the world is old, lad,
   And all the trees are brown,
And all the sport is stale, lad,
   And all the wheels run down ;
Creep home, and take your place there,
   The spent and maimed among ;
God grant you find one face there
   You loved when all was young."

ONE dull, late, winter afternoon Mr.
Mainwaring was riding slowly home towards Claybrooke. There had been a
frost the night before, which had given in
the morning, leaving the roads deep in
greasy yellow clay-mud. Long lines of
half-melted snow lay under the hedges on
the side away from the sun. The hedges
themselves were a hard purplish black in
the gathering dusk. The broad pasture-
lands looked brown and sad in the un-

certain light ; and the spaces of turf, on
either side the road, were coarse and boggy
from the wet, which stood in little dirty
pools every here and there. A bleak south-
easterly wind cried shrill through the bare
hawthorns and the scattered elm-trees,
promising more snow. It was a chilly
dreary evening, on which even a healthy
unimaginative man might well be affected
by the outward aspects of nature ; might
be full of gloomy fancies, and take depressing views of human nature and of
things in general.

Mr. Mainwaring had had a trying day,
and was a little disposed to think that
everything was " going to the bad." He
was chilled and somewhat tired ; but,
wishing to spare his horse, he jogged along
slowly up the muddy road under the broad
sweep of lowering gray sky. His head
was sunk into the collar of his coat, which
he had pulled up to keep off some of the
cold south-easterly wind ; his shoulders

were up to his ears ; he held the bridle
with stiff fingers ; both he and his big
chesnut hunter were splashed and plas-
tered with clay-mud from head to foot.
He had ridden a good way to the meet
in the morning, which had been bright
enough with pale winter sunshine; had seen
friends, and had a cheery time till about
one o'clock; then his horse cast a shoe, and
he had wasted some time seeking a black-
smith to put on another. When he came up
with the hounds again they were running,
and he had about a quarter of an hour's
gallop. They lost their fox, and moved off
to draw a distant covert; drew it blank;—
and about half-past three, with a snow-
storm gathering away down in the south-
east, Mr. Mainwaring found himself with a
good fourteen miles to ride home alone.

He was disgusted, too, with several
little social incidents in the day's work.
Not even fox-hunting seemed to him quite
a safe sport for an English gentleman in

these degenerate times, when the sons of
tradesmen, who had made all their money
in candles, or stockings, or soap, rode
better horses than he could afford to ride,
and treated him as an equal instead of a
superior.—Hardly treated him as an equal,
indeed, but rather as an antiquated and
behind-the-world sort of old gentleman,
who was by no means up to the level of
the civilisation of the present day. He
was specially incensed against a certain
young man of boisterous manners and of
a somewhat flashy appearance—nearly
related, it was said, to some well-known
London tobacconist — who had lately
settled in the neighbourhood, kept a lot
of horses, and hunted four or five days a
week. The young man in question happened to be particularly bumptious and
interfering by nature : but Mr. Mainwaring,
when annoyed, did not always take the
trouble to distinguish carefully between
the sins of the individual and those of the

class to which he belonged. He kindly accredited the race of retail tradesmen in general with the offences of this young man in particular, and condemned them all ; while the worst of it was, that Mr. Mainwaring could not deny that the fellow really rode hard, and had plenty of pluck.

"There's nothing left," he grumbled, " that a gentleman can do, without finding himself rubbing shoulders with half the shopkeepers in the country. What with a radical parliament and a radical press, the poor old country's going to the dogs as fast as it can. Fortunately my time won't be very long. I shall be safe in the churchyard before the worst of it comes, please God, but it's a bad look-out ahead —very bad."

It struck Mr. Mainwaring that his own life, looking back on it, was very like the history of that day. A cheery start in the morning sunshine ; a capital horse under him ; hope for the coming hours ;

plenty of friends ; a splendid burst for a
few minutes over the grass, when the pace
was hot and his blood tingled with healthy
excitement. Then pottering about the
dreary woodlands, in the chill mist, drawing and drawing for the fox that could
never be found ; and, at last, the long
lonely ride home in the cold and the
growing darkness. The day dying, the
sport all over, only the weariness and want
of success left. Dirty, tired, bespattered,
old,—that was what it all came to in the
end. Alas! for the pity of it !

Mr. Mainwaring stuck out his under lip
and set his teeth hard, bent his head a little
lower to avoid the bitter wind, and trotted
on, slowly and doggedly, up the muddy
road, with its wet strip of turf on either
hand, and bare, black, hawthorn hedges.

The hall at the Rectory, with a glowing
fire of great logs upon the hearth ; Bunton
waiting with dignified solicitude to attend
upon his master ; and Mrs. Mainwaring,

with her spotless cap, pretty little face, and tender wistful manner, coming forward in the ruddy light to welcome her beloved lord,—all these things were in most agreeable contrast to the sad, cold, gray night outside.

"I am too dirty to come near you, my dear," said Mr. Mainwaring, looking kindly at his wife. "I'll go into the study for ten minutes and get a good warm ; and then, Bunton, I'll have a hot bath in my dressing-room, before dinner.—We've had a wretched day," he added, as he followed Mrs. Mainwaring into the study. "The grass is as heavy as the plough ; and there seem to be no foxes in the country. Only had about ten minutes' gallop the whole day. Found a fox in Michael's Spinny, just the other side of the turnpike at Lowcote,—ran him into a drain on Staley's farm at Highthorne, and there was an end of the whole thing."

Mr. Mainwaring stood in front of the

study fire, with his hands under the tails
of his hunting-coat, stamping his feet to
get a little warmth into them, and thereby
plentifully besmearing the floor with the
half dry mud off his boots.

Mrs. Mainwaring abhorred a mess as
sincerely as Nature is said to abhor a
vacuum : but she was always too thankful
to get her husband home, safe and sound,
on these occasions, to make any objections
to the large supply of wet clay which he
invariably brought in with him.

"I am very sorry you have had such a
bad day," she said sympathetically ; and
then added after a pause, "Mrs. Adnitt
has been over here to-day. You remember Edward Dadley, don't you, Gerald ?"

"Yes, to be sure I do," said the Rector;
"and remember that he behaved like a fool
too. What about him ?"

"Oh! only Lucy Adnitt has been staying up in the north, and heard a good deal
about him. He has been away travelling

in America—shooting, I believe—for the last two years. He has just come back. He seems to have had a quarrel with his father about that cousin whom he wanted him to marry, you know. She's an heiress and the two estates join. Edward Dadley went away because of it."

"Just like old Dadley!" said Mr. Mainwaring bitterly. "I always thought he was a grasping fellow. His grandfather was a tradesman, and I suppose it's in the blood. The boy was well enough,—rather weak, perhaps, but I was fond of him. He behaved like an ass at last, though— his father's fault too, I daresay."

Mrs. Mainwaring, observing that her husband was not in a particularly urbane state of mind, seemed to think it well to change the conversation.

"Mr. Leeper is going to leave Lowcote," she remarked, a little inconsequently.

"That's a good riddance, any way,"

observed Mr. Mainwaring. "We can do very well without him here."

"He has got a large parish somewhere in the Black Country. The Adnitts are very anxious about the next presentation to the living at Lowcote."

"Why, it's not in their hands," said the Rector.

"No, but they think they might bring some influence to bear on the Bishop. Mrs. Adnitt asked me about Mr. Jones."

"Oh! Jones is a good creature enough," said Mr. Mainwaring a trifle contemptuously, stamping his feet again so that he showered mud liberally over the carpet. "But the old squire has an uncommonly hot tongue, you know, and if he talked much to Jones, as he can talk when he is put out, the poor fellow would be frightened clean out of his wits. They want a stronger man than Jones at Lowcote. Between ourselves, Susan, dear old Adnitt is a bit of a tyrant."

Poor Mrs. Mainwaring was fated on that evening, much against her will, to say things by no means calculated to soothe her husband. She moved away from the fireplace, and busied herself with putting some stray papers tidy on the study table.

"I find there has been some very unpleasant gossip going about Lowcote for some time," she said, without looking up. "I really hardly care to mention it, Gerald, but it annoyed me extremely."

"Really; why, what's the matter there?" asked Mr. Mainwaring. He was getting rather impatient; he wanted to go and have his hot bath.

"It seems that an extraordinary report has got abroad through Mr. Leeper saying something about Elizabeth."

"Good gracious!" Mr. Mainwaring exclaimed, thoroughly roused now, and interested. "What on earth can the man have to say about Elizabeth?"

"Oh! it may all be untrue, you know

Gerald," answered Mrs. Mainwaring quickly. " Mrs. Adnitt said it was only gossip. She only wanted to know whether we knew anything about it. There seems," she added, after a moment's pause, "to be a general impression that Mr. Leeper is very much—well, in fact, that he is in love with Elizabeth."

" God bless my soul !" cried the Rector. " Why, I'd as soon the child went and married a stake out of the hedge as that hard, lanky, bilious-looking fellow. What a piece of intolerable impertinence for him to think of such a thing !"

" But it mayn't be true, Gerald," said Mrs. Mainwaring, quite alarmed at the sudden storm she had raised.

" True ? " answered the Rector bitterly. " Anything may be true nowadays. All the old landmarks are going. Only to-day I learnt how much I was out of it all."

He felt again something of the distrust of the future, and contempt towards the present, that had troubled him on his lonely ride home. At that moment, it seemed to Mr. Mainwaring a not unfitting conclusion to the day's work that Mr. Leeper—whom he most cordially disliked—should become his nephew, and eventually step into his shoes at Claybrooke. " The old order " was changing, he felt, more every day ; and he belonged to the old order. Mr. Mainwaring had a sense upon him, sometimes, that the world was walking right away from him, and that he was fighting sadly—at moments almost half-heartedly — in a lost cause. The old-fashioned country gentleman, with all his old kindly, rather unimaginative system of things, was slowly giving way, he feared, before the new age of so-called progress, and culture, and art.

But the Rector was tired and stiff and chilly; he could not meditate for any long space of time, under existing circumstances, even upon the doubtfulness of his own

position in the general economy of things.
He turned to his wife after a moment, and
asked more sadly than angrily—

"Did he see her often, Susan?"

"No, no, not very often, I think, when
she was here last," answered Mrs. Mainwaring.

She was trying hard to remember: but
she was a little confused and agitated,
first by the vehemence and now by the
sadness of her husband's manner. She
had a good memory for small events, but
the meetings in question had taken place
more than a year before, and it was slightly
difficult to recall them accurately.

"He called here once—I think it was
only once—when you were away in July;
and we met him again at the Adnitts'
afterwards. There he talked a good deal
to Elizabeth."

"Oh! well," said the Rector, who found
this piece of information decidedly reassuring, "that does not amount to very

much. You contradicted it all to Mrs. Adnitt, I suppose?"

"Yes, I spoke very strongly," answered Mrs. Mainwaring. "But you see, Gerald, for a long while I have not had Elizabeth's full confidence."

The Rector was always disposed to advance pretty rapidly to the defence of his niece. He could hardly believe that she would lend herself, in any way, to help work out an evil destiny for him.

"If I know anything of Elizabeth, Susan," he said quickly, "she would soon let Mr. Leeper know he was making a considerable mistake, if he spoke to her on this subject."

"I cannot pretend to say what Elizabeth might do," answered Mrs. Mainwaring rather stiffly. She was now and then somewhat jealous of her husband's confidence in his niece. "I only know that this report is annoying—most annoying to me."

" Well," said the Rector, influenced by
three considerations—first, by the hope-
lessness of fighting against his fate, however
unpleasant that fate might be ; secondly,
by the sense that he and his wife were
beginning to tread on rather dangerous
ground ; and thirdly, by a growing desire
for his hot bath—" Well, it is a nuisance ;
but I daresay people will forget the whole
thing in a few days. I daresay Mrs.
Adnitt made the most of it.—There, I
really am so stiff I must go. Don't vex
yourself about it, Susie, any more. I'll
think it over, and we'll talk about it some
other time. Oh ! by the way," he added,
turning back for a moment, just as he
was going out of the study door, " can't
we have dinner a quarter of an hour
sooner ? "

CHAPTER III.

" L'opinion dispose de tout.　Elle fait la beauté, la
justice, et le bonheur, qui est le tout du monde."

MRS. FRANK LORIMER was not naturally
of a patient disposition ; and when the
progress of events was not altogether as
rapid as she desired, she had a strong inclination to help it forward with a private
shove. She thoroughly enjoyed the exercise of personal power which she was
sensible of in thus hurrying conclusions ;
and, having an ingenious mind, she generally found convincing arguments for proving that her interference was both necessary
and legitimate.　It is a great temptation
to women of a certain temperament to
play freely with the souls of their acquaintances, and to try to force the hand of

destiny concerning them. By carefully
ignoring the tricks they lose, and rather
ostentatiously counting up those they take,
these good ladies contrive generally to
create, both in their own minds and in
the minds of the onlookers, an impression
of continuous and remarkable success in
the playing of their rather dangerous game.

Mrs. Frank Lorimer had watched the
course of Elizabeth and Fred Wharton's
friendship with sincere interest. It had
supplied a certain element of refined excitement in her daily life which she
relished keenly. She had continually
been aware of the situation, she expected
it would develop: but though Wharton
seemed to be growing somewhat preoccupied, and though Elizabeth, at times, was
restless and capricious, Mrs. Frank had
candidly to confess that the situation did
not develop appreciably. She began to
get a little impatient. It seemed to her
they must have drunk the cup of friend-

ship pretty well to the dregs; and she was convinced that, in the case of a friendship between a man and a woman, love is at the bottom of the cup, just as surely as Truth is at the bottom of the proverbial well. Mrs. Frank wanted something to happen; she really quite yawned for a change of scene.

No sooner had she fairly acknowledged her own sense of *ennui* in face of the present state of things, than the most excellent reasons for doing her best to alter that state of things began to crowd in upon her. For some time past she had been conscious that Elizabeth's intimacy with Fred Wharton had provoked a good deal of comment. People observed rather curiously upon the fact that whenever they called upon Elizabeth Lorimer, " that young Mr. Wharton was sure to be there." One or two people had asked Mrs. Frank point-blank whether there was " anything in it;" and, when she answered in a vague

and airy manner, had put up their eyebrows with an appearance of slight
surprise. One excellent and well-intentioned old lady, who affected propriety as
decidedly as she relished scandal, had
intimated so undisguisedly that she considered the connection a peculiar one,
that Mrs. Frank felt a growing conviction
regarding the absolute duty of prompt
interference.

Fanny Lorimer had decided long ago
that Elizabeth must marry again. She
had gone further, and decided that she
must marry Fred Wharton ; she thought
they would suit admirably, and be very
happy together. Elizabeth's superfluous
enthusiasms would be nicely moderated
by Wharton's philosophic calm ; while he
would be stimulated to greater earnestness
of purpose by his wife's strong and ardent
sympathies. It was a charming arrangement undoubtedly; and there was just that
spice of malice about the conception of

it, which made it specially attractive to Fanny Lorimer's mind. She could not forgive Wharton's apparent indifference to love and marriage ; his perfect immunity from all those daily cares and vexations, which seem to be the necessary result of the close relationship of two imperfect human creatures. She felt it would be wonderfully refreshing to reduce him to the ordinary level ; to see him chained to the oar like the rest of us ; to hear him crying out that the shoe pinched, now and then ; to watch him hopping mildly about with clipped wings, instead of flying gaily hither and thither as fancy fired. She was sensible that Wharton clearly perceived the limitations and short-comings of her own character; and though she liked him very well—in a way,—she never could forgive him this keenness of insight. It would be extremely exhilarating to get the better of him for once.

She was just a little bit afraid of Eliza-

beth ; if the progress of events was to be
hastened, and the hand of destiny to be
forced, Fanny Lorimer felt she dared not
attempt to attain her end by means of
Elizabeth. If she was to administer a
shove to the situation, it must be administered through Fred Wharton. Yet, with
all her audacity, she did not quite care
to undertake the business single-handed.
She would like, if possible, to be backed
by her husband's approval.

Now unfortunately—or perhaps fortunately—Frank Lorimer hated diplomacy.
He cultivated the very erroneous notion—
so it appeared to his wife—that every one
really knew his, or her, own business best.
He strongly objected to interfering. He
objected both to the trouble and to the
responsibility of interfering : but he had a
deeper feeling on the subject, as well, and
one which Fanny Lorimer was perhaps
hardly capable of appreciating. He had
a certain reverence for the mysterious in-

dividuality of each human being, which
made it seem to him almost sacrilegious to
attempt to arrange or modify the future in
any way for them.   Frank Lorimer was
not what is generally understood by the
term "a religious-minded man"—far from
it : but he believed deeply in a kind, and
yet awful Providence, which shapes the
life of every man, and he feared to run
counter to the purposes of that tremendous
power with any impertinent and short-
sighted plans and fancies of his own.

Fanny Lorimer's pretty little head was
full of schemes for the silencing of adverse
criticism, the subduing of Fred Wharton,
and the settling of all difficulties regarding
Elizabeth by means of this marriage, one
evening when she and her husband were
—for a wonder—dining alone together.
That afternoon she had been a good deal
disturbed by the questions concerning her
sister-in-law's relations with Wharton, that
had been put to her by different people.

She had quite persuaded herself that the present state of things could not be permitted to go on. She saw clearly that something really must be done at once ; but she wanted her husband's sanction for the doing of it ; and she knew that, under the circumstances, it would be safer to try to obtain his sanction by a little management than to ask for it openly.

The parlour-maid had just left the room, and Frank was refreshing himself with a peaceful cigarette before going upstairs. He and his wife were sitting opposite to each other : but there was a large flowering plant in the centre of the table which acted as a pretty effectual screen between them. Fanny Lorimer, having a delicate mission to perform, regarded this as a not wholly unfortunate circumstance.

"I am rather worried about Elizabeth, Frank," she began quietly.

"Why ?" he inquired. " I'm sure she

was looking uncommonly well when I saw her the day before yesterday."

"Oh yes! perfectly well in health," answered Fanny Lorimer, drawing a little pattern slowly on the white table-cloth with the blade of her silver dessert knife. "She's quite well, but she is moody and uncertain. I'm not surprised," she added after a moment—as Frank did not answer—looking up with a charming air of candour which, owing to the intervening plant, was unfortunately lost upon her husband. "I don't wonder at it the least; any nice woman would be moody in her position. I never supposed she could exist for very long merely on blue china and ideas."

"I wish you'd let the children come down to dessert, Fanny," remarked Frank rather complainingly. "I don't see them all day because I'm out, and then in the evening I'm always told they're in bed and asleep."

"Well, if you insist on dining at a quarter to eight, Frank," she answered with some decision, "you can't expect to have the children at dessert. Imagine how wretchedly pasty Nini would look if she sat up till this hour! Next to a lot of money, a good complexion is the best fortune in the world for a girl. Nini's complexion shan't be spoilt for want of sleep, any way, I'm determined."

"It's a bore, all the same," said Frank, turning his chair side-ways so as to lean one elbow on the table, and stretching his legs out comfortably before him.

This change of position on his part prevented the plant acting so effectually as a screen : but Fanny Lorimer was not wanting in courage, nor was she easily turned from any purpose that she had set her mind on.

"I really almost wish sometimes," she said, bending her head down, while she carefully elaborated the pattern on the table-cloth — "I really do quite wish sometimes that Elizabeth would marry again."

Frank Lorimer glanced up quickly, with a touch of displeasure on his pleasant, good-looking face.

"It is hardly two years since Robert died, Fanny," he said. "It would be rather soon, don't you think?"

"Oh! pray don't imagine I like second marriages," she said, looking up too, and speaking rapidly. "You know perfectly well, Frank, that I think them absolutely detestable—only allowed for the hardness of our hearts, you know. But then Elizabeth has got no children, you see, and no near relations except ourselves and those tiresome, narrow-minded, old Mainwarings."

She paused a moment, and then added with a certain touch of unwillingness, which was very becoming :—

"And Elizabeth is rather peculiar, too ; she is not quite careful enough ; she makes people talk about her. Really, you know, Frank, your friend Mr. Wharton is always there; and of course people can't help observing it."

Frank Lorimer was silent. The conversation was thoroughly distasteful to him. He felt a little irritated with his charming wife; and yet, in fairness, he had to admit, that there might be a good deal of truth in what she said.

Fanny Lorimer added a few flourishes to her pattern on the table-cloth. She wanted her last remarks to have time to sink well down into her husband's mind.

"Do you want Fred to marry her then?" asked Frank rather sharply at last. He did not look, somehow, as if he relished the idea at all.

"Oh! I don't know," she answered, with a delicate shrug of her shoulders. "It wouldn't be much use wanting Mr. Wharton to marry anybody, you know. He likes to drift. He hates taking steps; proposing to Elizabeth would be taking a great step, I fancy. But still his being there so much is annoying. It leads to all sorts of misconceptions. It really is rather compromising for Elizabeth, you know."

Fanny Lorimer said the last few words with a delightful little air of sorrowful conviction.

This was very unpleasant, Frank thought, if it really was true. Wharton had been a great deal at Elizabeth's lately, he knew; therefore he was afraid it might be true. Frank Lorimer disliked unpleasant things immensely ; he always tried to avoid any lengthened discussion of them. He got up hastily, knocking the long ash of his cigarette off on to the carpet. This caused Fanny Lorimer an instant of acute misery : but she dominated her domestic sensations with heroic fortitude. The carpet must be sacrificed, she felt, to the situation.

" If it's really compromising, some one ought to tell him so," Frank said.

" Do you mean that, really, Frank ? "
asked his wife, getting up too, and letting
the handle of her dessert knife fall with a
gentle thud upon the table-cloth.

"Oh! I don't know," he answered testily.
" For goodness' sake, Fanny, let the subject alone and we'll go upstairs."

Fanny Lorimer was absolutely delightful
during the rest of the evening. Her husband imagined she was prettily repentant
for having introduced disagreeable subjects
of conversation after dinner ; and thought
it very nice that she should have such a
tender conscience where his comfort was
concerned. One really has a great respect
for the Serpent sometimes. He must have
been wonderfully subtle to have beguiled
Eve ; or else the first woman must have
been curiously less acute than her daughters
of the last few centuries ! Frank Lorimer
was beautifully innocent of his wife's intentions; and Fanny Lorimer was radiant, for
she saw a clear path before her.

Fortune is said to favour the brave. Fortune certainly in this case favoured Mrs. Frank Lorimer. In the usual course of events she did not often find herself alone with Mr. Wharton ; but it so happened that, within a week after the above conversation, she had an excellent opportunity for administering just that little impetus to the forward movement of events that she had so earnestly coveted.

She called one afternoon at her sister-in-law's, wishing to make some arrangement regarding the entertaining of one or two friends. Martha, in answer to her inquiries, announced that Elizabeth was not at home ; she would not be in for half an hour or so. But, Martha added, Mr. Wharton, who was also anxious to see her mistress, was awaiting her return upstairs. Here, then, was Fanny Lorimer's opportunity ; all the circumstances perfectly arranged, the path smoothed for her, and—supposing Eliza-

beth did not return sooner than she was
expected to—the most admirable occasion
for her to express her sisterly fears to Fred
Wharton. Fanny Lorimer, of course, was
glad ; and yet she could not disguise from
herself that she felt a little nervous. However, after a moment's indecision, she con-
cluded that she could never respect herself
again if she gave way to vague alarms,
and retired from the performance of this,
her obvious duty. She, too, would wait
for Elizabeth's return.

"I know my way ; you need not
trouble to come up with me," she said
graciously to Martha. Then she walked
quietly upstairs, and went, unannounced,
into the drawing-room.

Fred Wharton was beguiling the time,
during which he waited for his fair hostess,
by playing. The piano had been placed
in the back drawing-room, and was in a
position which, even had he been less
absorbed in his present occupation, would

have prevented his seeing Mrs. Frank as she came into the room. She, on her part, wanted a few minutes for quiet reflection ; she wanted to arrange the manner of her attack. She felt that some people might think her just a trifle mean for taking advantage of Wharton's musical enthusiasm in this way: but the end, surely, might very well justify the means. She settled herself in a comfortable corner and waited patiently for the music to cease before she should speak. The *portière* between the two rooms was partly drawn aside, and by leaning a little forward Mrs. Frank could just see Wharton as he sat at the piano.

As we have already noted, Wharton's nature always seemed to grow deeper and more earnest when he was playing. On this occasion, owing perhaps to certain new feelings which were beginning to stir within him, perhaps only to the fact that he believed himself to be alone and unob-

served, he seemed to be speaking the very
depths of his being out in the music.

Fortunately Fanny Lorimer's nature
was not easily influenced by outbursts of
feeling, otherwise she might easily have
forgotten her purpose while listening to
Wharton's stormy playing, and have lost
herself on an ocean of fancy and of wild
desire for some fair and unknown good.
Fanny Lorimer had a small head, but
she contrived never to lose it; consequently she just sat still and matured her
little plans, with a fine indifference to her
surroundings.

Suddenly Wharton left off abruptly in ·
the middle of a tempestuous passage, and,
after playing a few chords softly, fell to
humming the melancholy song that had
so overset Elizabeth the first time she
heard it.   He sang the words of the
last verse out loud, with a certain quiet
suggestion of regret and sorrow that almost startled Mrs. Frank.   She had not

a very delicate sense of honour, but there was a touch of self-revelation in Wharton's singing, which seemed to her clearly not intended for unsympathetic ears. It made her uncomfortable; she did not like to listen any longer ; also, she began to be afraid that Elizabeth might come back, and that her opportunity would be lost. She managed to get up with a great rustling of skirts, half overset her chair, and save it hastily from actually falling, with a rapid movement, and sharp little exclamation, which effectually attracted Wharton's attention.

He turned round quickly, expecting to see Elizabeth ; and his face did not take an altogether agreeable expression when he perceived who it was that had interrupted him.

"Ah ! my dear Mr. Wharton, forgive me !" cried Mrs. Frank, coming towards him with an outstretched hand and one of her peculiarly brilliant smiles. "I am

so accustomed to running in and out of
this house, without any parade of servants
announcing me, that I came in quietly
just now, and I'm afraid I have taken you
by surprise. I really could not interrupt
you at first, you were playing so deliciously.
That tiresome chair nearly fell over. Ah!"
she added, advancing towards the piano,
" what lovely flowers."

On the top of the piano lay a great
bunch of white roses, stephanotis, and
lilies of the valley. Mrs. Frank put out
her hand, picked up the bouquet, and
almost buried her pretty face among the
clustering blossoms.

"Ah! how perfectly delicious they
are," she said. "Are they destined for
my fortunate sister-in-law?"

"Mrs. Lorimer is very fond of white
flowers," said Wharton rather loftily.

He had an uncomfortable sense of being
taken at a disadvantage somehow. He
had been feeling a little excited ; and just

because he so very seldom felt really excited
he had a difficulty in regaining his usual
calm manner, getting his social armour
on again, and meeting Mrs. Frank with
weapons as sharp, and yet as dainty, as
her own, in the battlefield of ordinary conversation. He had an absurd misgiving
that something unpleasant was impend-
ing; and that he would not find himself
equal to the occasion.

"Oh! they are perfectly delicious," said
Mrs. Frank, smelling the flowers again.
"Have you any idea, Mr. Wharton, when
Elizabeth will be in?"

"She will be in in time for tea, I suppose," answered Wharton.

He was rather offended with Mrs. Frank
Lorimer; and there was something uncomfortable, to his thinking, in the way she
seemed to take for granted that he knew
all about Elizabeth's movements.

"That won't be just yet," said Mrs.
Frank. Then she added, looking up at

him with an air of admirable candour, " I
am very glad we have met here, Mr.
Wharton, for I really wanted to see you
very much."

Wharton did not feel inclined to make
a pretty speech, so he merely bowed his
acknowledgments of her complimentary
desires. A silent bow from a person one
knows very well is hardly an encouraging
thing : but Mrs. Frank was apparently by
no means abashed.

" It may sound very strange," she continued, " but I wanted to say something
to you about my sister-in-law. It may
seem unusual, but then you know her so
very well. I think you will understand
my motives."

Wharton was standing near the piano,
with his back to the window ; Mrs. Frank
was opposite to him, with the light
falling full upon her. Somehow he mis-
trusted the expression of her innocent
little face ; and he disliked her taking

possession of his offering of white flowers, and holding them so composedly in her hand while she talked to him. Wharton had a fanciful feeling upon him that she would keep those flowers, and that he should never give them to Elizabeth after all.

There was a pause. Fanny Lorimer began arranging her bonnet-strings with one hand. This occasioned her to turn her head a little on one side, so that she no longer looked her companion full in the face.

"My sister-in-law's position is such a peculiar one," she went on, after a minute or two. "She is so young, and so unusually handsome ; and of course people observe her a good deal, and talk about her. People will say odious unpleasant things about every one, and of course she doesn't escape. I really do wish sometimes, Mr. Wharton, you know, that Elizabeth would be just a little more careful and conventional."

Wharton had not the smallest desire to discuss Elizabeth thus.

"Mrs. Lorimer is perfectly capable of taking care of her own reputation, I should imagine," he said stiffly.

"Ah! no, there you're mistaken," answered Mrs. Frank quickly; and there was something so entirely straightforward and genuine in her manner as she spoke, that Wharton felt considerably mollified towards her. "It is stupid, cold-hearted, worldly-minded creatures like me who are perfectly capable of taking care of their own reputations. Elizabeth really is too simple, and honest, and noble-hearted, to think what people will say about her, when she does this or that. She is too innocent; and the consequence is that she lands herself in all manner of bothers. She has ideas, you know, about life, and ideas are always fatal. The world seems to me," added Mrs. Frank, giving a final little pat to her bonnet-strings and looking straight in front of her abstractedly,—"the world seems to me to be divided into clever people with ideas and stupid people without them ;—and the latter have to spend three parts of their time in fishing the former out of their difficulties. I need not say I belong to the stupid section, and "—she looked up at Wharton suddenly—" I am absolutely on thorns about my sister-in-law just now."

" Really, indeed," said Wharton coldly, " why ?"

Mrs. Frank Lorimer stepped aside into the shadow of the heavy window curtains. She was going to play her highest card, and it made her feel a little nervous ; she was afraid of appearing too much interested or excited. Wharton, she felt sure, was watching her carefully. She knew that with some men what she was about to say would have exactly the contrary effect to that which she desired to produce : but she trusted to an almost quixotic strain of honour which she had observed once or twice in Wharton. He would rather do anything than lose the least jot or tittle of his self-respect.

" I will tell you why," she said, smelling the flowers again ; "and I shall have to say something extremely disagreeable. I shall offend your taste horribly. I really doubt whether you will ever forgive me : but I must consider Elizabeth, you know."

She paused—it really was an odious thing to say. She wondered what Wharton would do?—she wondered what Frank would think?—fortunately he would only hear her version of the story,—Wharton would be very certain not to mention it!

" In point of fact, then, you come here too often, Mr. Wharton," she said.

There are moments when it is quite impossible to maintain an appearance of philosophic calm. Wharton was pretty well master of himself on most occasions : but just now he could not manage to con-

ceal his feelings. He blushed violently,
and that added most materially to his
sense of anger and wretchedness.

Mrs. Frank Lorimer did not give him
time to speak.

" Yes," she said quickly, looking at him
with an air of becoming distraction, and
stretching out her hands—flowers and all
—with a charmingly appealing gesture.
" It is a horrible thing to say to you.
You can never forgive me. I have outraged your taste, I know, and entirely disgusted you. But then people will talk,
and there is nobody to tell you but me.
Speaking is forced upon me — I really
cannot help myself."

" This is extremely painful," said Wharton. " I am more than sorry that I should
have caused you any annoyance, or in
any way—really it is too unpleasant," he
added angrily, turning away.

" Pray, pray remember," cried Mrs.
Frank hastily, coming a step nearer to

him, and speaking imploringly,—" pray remember that Elizabeth knows nothing of all this,—is absolutely ignorant of it. She positively knows nothing of it."

Wharton stood looking down. Perhaps he had never felt so thoroughly uncomfortable in all his life before. He had been trying delicate and philosophic experiments as he supposed ; and the world at large was accusing him, all the while, of an ordinary stupid bit of indiscretion. The position seemed to him intolerably vulgar. He felt enraged with himself, enraged with Fanny Lorimer, enraged with the whole universe. He had got entangled—·yes, that was what people were saying—with Mrs. Lorimer. He could fancy the way this and that and the other person talked him over, and laughed, as they each added their little quota of gossip to the heap. And he had always kept himself so free of this sort of thing. Oh, it really was too odious ! Heavens and earth, what a fool he had been, and what a wretchedly commonplace scrape he had got himself into!

Just then Elizabeth came in from her walk. Mrs. Frank and Wharton heard her shut the front door, and come lightly and quickly up the stairs. They stood together, in the shady back drawing-room, with its soft dusky colours and quaint furniture, feeling like two suddenly discovered conspirators.

CHAPTER IV.

"Looking up, I saw it was a starling hung in a little
   cage.—'I can't get out, I can't get out,' said the
   starling."

ELIZABETH certainly looked very handsome as she came into the room. She
still wore nothing but black : but within
the last few months she had taken to
dressing in a rather superb manner. This
afternoon she had been paying some visits,
and was arrayed in a gown of some rich
material, loaded with shimmering jet
trimmings, which glanced and glittered
as she moved. Her mantle — fitting
tightly over the shoulders and showing
the lines of the bust—matched her gown,
and was bordered with deep, soft, black
fur. She had on a little fluffy French
bonnet, tying with broad strings under

the chin,—the extreme becomingness of which had thrown Fanny Lorimer into a small ecstasy of envy and admiration the first time she saw it. Perhaps Elizabeth's style of dress was more suitable to a woman of forty than to a girl of barely four-and-twenty : but it had the effect of making her look younger, and not older, than her real age.

Mrs. Frank had a gift for receiving rapid impressions. She glanced up at her sister-in-law as she entered the room, and said to herself—

"Certainly Elizabeth is wonderfully distinguished looking."

Wharton glanced up at her too. He was sensible of a sharp feeling of longing and regret. He was not at all under the impression that he was what is technically called "in love" with Elizabeth Lorimer,— he was utterly uncertain about the future : —but he knew that their pleasant friend- ship was at an end, any way. Mrs. Frank

had just given it its *coup de grâce*. Nothing,
absolutely nothing, could put things back
on their old easy footing again.

Wharton had nothing to say ; he stood
silent, feeling contemptibly wretched.
Fanny Lorimer was the first to regain her
presence of mind, and moved forward to
meet her sister-in-law with a rather unnecessarily brilliant smile.

Elizabeth, quite unconscious of all the
plots against her peace, took Mrs. Frank's
hand, and then turning to Wharton, said
cordially—

"How nice of you both to wait for me.
What delicious flowers, Fanny ; where
did you get them ? Oh ! you've been
playing," she added, turning again to
Wharton ; "have you brought that thing
of Schumann's you promised me ? Come
into the other room and let us have
some tea, and then you shall play it to
me. I really want refreshment ; I have
been paying such a lot of tiresome visits."

Elizabeth began unfastening her mantle as she spoke. She stood there looking very sweet and gracious in her shimmering dress.

"I'm afraid I can't stay now," said Wharton hastily, and—he knew it only too well—awkwardly, without looking at her.

Elizabeth opened her eyes rather wide with surprise, and paused, holding the half-unfastened fronts of her mantle in either hand. She was arrested by something unusual in Wharton's manner; it was so unlike him to refuse to do anything that she asked him to do.

"I ought really to have gone before," said he again. And then added vindictively, "I should have gone before, but that I have been so enchained with Mrs. Frank Lorimer's delightful conversation."

Fanny Lorimer winced a little; this was the form his resentment was going to take, then!

"I am afraid I must go," repeated Wharton, looking at Elizabeth almost sadly.

"How very odd," she said, with a sudden sense of chill and discomfort. "You have waited for me till now, and then, directly I come in, you rush away in this strange fashion."

Elizabeth went on unfastening her mantle.

"Pray don't let us detain you," she added rather stiffly.

"You can't know how sorry I am that I am obliged to go, Mrs. Lorimer," said Wharton impetuously and rather incoherently.

But he offered no further explanation, and Elizabeth shook hands with him coldly. She was annoyed; she could not understand it all.

Fanny Lorimer had turned away, and was fidgeting with some loose music on the piano. She was in a small fever of vexation. Wharton seemed to her to be behaving with a wretched want of presence of mind. What would be the upshot of it? Had she, after all, made a great mistake?

There was a pause. Fanny Lorimer heard Wharton shut the door; and then as Elizabeth flung down her mantle, with a rustle of silk and clash of beads, she turned round.

"What is the matter with him, Fanny?" said Elizabeth hastily. She looked disturbed and bewildered.

"Oh! my dear, I suppose he has moods, and fads, and fancies, like the rest of us," answered Mrs. Frank, coming forward and shrugging her shoulders with a touch of irritation. "Pray don't require reasons from me for the eccentric doings of the young men of our acquaintance, for I own myself quite incapable, as a rule, of discovering any. The ways of man are utterly incomprehensible, in my humble opinion."

Fanny Lorimer certainly felt better
when she had delivered herself of this
attack on mankind in general. If circumstances will not allow of your actually
injuring an obnoxious individual, there is
always a distinct degree of comfort to be
derived from throwing a few stones at the
whole race. Fanny Lorimer could have
found it in her heart to run red-hot
bodkins into Wharton at this moment:
but, as there are prejudices against such
practical expressions of personal feeling
in the present day, she refreshed herself
with a little general abuse of his sex. Then
she looked up quite serenely at Elizabeth,
and said—

"By the way, I believe he brought
these flowers for you, Elizabeth. I picked
them up while we were talking; and
then, either I forgot to give them back
to him, or he forgot to ask for them;
any way, here they are."

Elizabeth glanced at the flowers for a

moment, as Mrs. Frank held them out to
her.

"I think you had better keep them,"
she said. "They seem to belong to you
more than to me. And they are really
too sweet, they make the room quite
oppressive. No, I don't want them," she
added.

Fred Wharton was in a very unenvi-
able state of mind as he left Mrs. Lorimer's house and walked slowly home
towards Chelsea. He had a conviction
that some of the pleasantest days of his
life were over for ever. He regretted the
past ; he was acutely uncomfortable in
the present ; and he distrusted the future.
It was a miserable predicament for a
young man, who had been wont to pride
himself on his perfect serenity of mind
and on the delightful security of his position, to find himself in.

Wharton meditated upon the situation
all that evening : but, look at it which

way he might, there was a lion in the
path. On every side he seemed beset
with dangers and difficulties. He felt
he could not meet Elizabeth again until
he knew his own mind and had decided
on some positive plan of action. On
the other hand, it was almost impossible to remain in London without meeting her. And she, at least, had not done
him any wrong ; how could he neglect
and avoid her, without giving the slightest
reason for his conduct ? Finally, he decided on the safe but unheroic course of
running away. He felt he must have
time to think the matter calmly out ; he
entirely refused to be hurried towards any
premature conclusion. So next morning
he telegraphed to a bachelor friend in
Sussex, who had a delightful house, and
a delightful habit of letting his guests do
very much what they pleased, without
making any too strenuous efforts at entertaining them. Wharton telegraphed to

this convenient individual, saying that he was out of sorts and "wanted a rest;" and receiving a prompt reply from Adolphus Carr—the friend in question—to the effect that he would be entirely welcome, he set off without further delay.

He had cherished a sort of hope that once away from London, and from the observant eyes of his friends and acquaintances, he should find his difficulties melt away. He had a sort of hope that the windy March weather, the great stretches of turf-clad down, with that delicate strip of silver sea on the southern horizon, would act as a moral tonic upon him, and fill him with clear and distinct desires and resolutions. But he was disappointed. Nature seemed curiously indifferent to the perturbations and distresses of this pleasant young gentleman, with his philosophic and imaginative temperament, his questionings and uncertainties, and his charmingly

furnished rooms down in Chelsea. She
was altogether too busy with storm and
sunshine, and the mysterious processes of
birth, and growth, and failure, and death,
and decay, to have any spare time to read
him private lessons of fortitude or wisdom.
She is no respecter of persons, indeed, and
seems to care no more tenderly for the
needs of the most talented of her human
children, than for the grass and daisies they
thoughtlessly crush under their feet.

Perhaps Wharton looked at the position
with unnecessary seriousness: but he had
always been so engaged in watching other
people that he had, so far, done very
little living on his own account. As Mrs.
Frank said, he hated taking steps ; and
he doubly hated being forced by outside
opinion to take them.   If only things had
been left alone, Wharton thought, they
would have arranged themselves : but to
propose to Elizabeth Lorimer because
certain busybodies chose to say that he

ought to do so, seemed to him utterly
monstrous. All his old objections to
marrying came upon him with overwhelm-
ing force. He liked Elizabeth Lorimer
immensely ; liked her better, he owned to
himself, than he had ever liked any woman
before : but then he liked so many other
things as well,—his friends, his freedom,
his art. If he only liked Elizabeth either
rather more or rather less, it seemed to
him that he should know better what to
do. As it was, he turned the matter this
way and that, over and over again, and
found himself as far from a decision as
ever.

Wharton's very mental acuteness made
him cowardly and uncertain. The possible results of every plan of action fairly
frightened him. He had no instinct to
fall back upon ; it was all a weighing, and
balancing, and measuring of probabilities,
and possibilities, and desirabilities, without
any strong and compelling current of feel-

ing to draw or drive him in any particular direction.   His mental compass
seemed to be depolarised ; the needle
no longer swung true.   He wanted supremely to do what was right and honour-
able : but for the life of him, he could not
see exactly which course right and honour
commanded him to adopt.

A simpler-minded man, like Mr. Mainwaring, or—in a lesser degree—like Frank
Lorimer, would have asked himself one or
two straightforward questions and abided
by the result.   Had he really compromised
the young lady, Frank would have asked
himself, and if so what must he do?
Obviously give her an opportunity of
refusing him, to put the matter in a
modest form.   And if she accepted him?
—Well, after all, whether he wanted to
marry or not, chance would have provided
him with a very charming wife ; he must
be thankful, and put his predilections for
celibacy in his pocket.

But Fred Wharton could not approach the matter in this direct way. He had lost his sense of distinct light and shade, so to speak, in his observation of local colour. He objected to talking about right and wrong; right and wrong, to his seeing, were modified and blended by a thousand side-lights and accidents of position, which made it impossible fairly to disentangle them. He was so anxious to see Truth from every point of view, that he spent all his time in revolving round and round her, changing his standing-ground continually; instead — like a practical man—of clutching boldly at the nearest fold of her flowing garments, and holding on to that determinedly. In short, like nearly all highly sensitive and imaginative persons, Wharton, having for a moment lost his mental balance, was disposed entirely to mistake the relative value of things; and while he was engaged in sedulously straining at a

gnat, ran great risk of swallowing a whole
caravan of camels.

Behind all these other feelings, there lingered an absurd but haunting idea that in
marrying Elizabeth he would be spoiling
a great artistic effect. He did not like
to think of her settling down and assum-
ing the *rôle* of an ordinary respectable
commonplace matron. It seemed to him
that she would lose a great deal of her
charm under those circumstances. He had
accepted Mrs. Frank's notion concerning
Elizabeth, as has already been mentioned.
He had been waiting and looking out for
a long time for a dramatic *dénouement;*
and he could not help feeling that Elizabeth would be somewhat of a fraud if the
dénouement did not come off. She seemed
to him cut out for some striking, perhaps tragic, situation; and he thought it
would certainly be a loss to have her sink
down to the usual dead level of woman-
hood. On the other hand, there would be

something rather distracting about a wife who might develop suddenly any day and surprise you immensely. It seemed to Wharton a little like undertaking a Jack-in-the-box with an insecure fastening, and he could not imagine any possession less conducive to domestic peace and security. These and a dozen more puzzling thoughts occurred to Wharton, as he wandered over the short-cropped turf of the chalk downs in the blustering March weather. At last, when nearly three weeks had passed away, he began to be aware that his position and attitude of mind were rapidly becoming extremely ludicrous. This state of things could not go on for ever. Adolphus Carr was expecting a house full of people, and Wharton was sensible that he was just a little in the way. As both reason and desire refused to lead him, he determined to fall back on what undevout persons call "chance," and devout ones call Providence. He would

go back to London ; perhaps some un-
looked-for contingency—perhaps the mere
sight of Elizabeth might make the way
clear. Wharton did not wish to have too
good a reason for laughing at himself ;
and he felt that his flight and long-con-
tinued state of uncertainty had an element
of absurdity in them:—too, he remembered
some drawing engagements that he could
no longer neglect. He must hope that
"something would turn up."

The rooms overlooking the river presented a very inviting appearance, after
the chilly desolate country shivering
in the cool embraces of early spring.
Wharton's spirits rose. Something certainly, he thought, would turn up to help
him out of his difficulties. Meanwhile
events had been taking place in London
which had considerably changed the
aspect of Elizabeth Lorimer's affairs.

CHAPTER V.

"Comment, disaient-ils,
Enchanter les belles
Sans philtres subtils?"

THERE comes a moment in the history of the life of each of the saints, when Satan, baffled at all other points, makes one last and desperate assault upon the soul through the medium of the senses. St. Anthony could not escape from this trial in the burning solitude of the Egyptian desert, nor St. Francis amid the spotless purity of the alpine snows, nor St. Benedict in his cave among the cruel rocks and briars. Nor could poor Mr. Leeper escape it either, though he had a yellowish complexion and sparse black beard; and though he lived in this enlightened nineteenth century, when, as we know, "the sea of faith" is no

longer " at the full," and we only listen—
some sadly and some gladly—to "its
melancholy, long, withdrawing roar," re-
treating "down the vast edges," and
" naked shingles of the world."

Without asserting that Mr. Leeper, at
this or any other stage of his career, deserved the honours of canonisation, we must
allow that, having taken no small pains to
form himself upon the orthodox models, he
had a perfect right to suffer all the orthodox temptations. It may be added that
the natural man dies very hard in each one
of us; perhaps fortunately, for if it had not
always been so,—if the said natural man
had not always been blessed with a considerable amount of vitality,—there is no
saying in how many more wonderful vaga-
ries the human race might not have already
indulged, or how much farther away we
might not have wandered, by this time,
from our great mother Nature, and from
the simple foundations of our humanity.

During the year and more that had passed since Elizabeth Lorimer left Claybrooke, Mr. Leeper had by no means ceased to think of the stately, gray-eyed, young lady with whom—from many points of view—a nearer connection appeared so desirable. Mr. Leeper's mind was of a very tenacious order. When he had once conceived an idea, it was pretty sure eventually to influence his action in some direct and practical way. His was not a poetical mind, in which a thousand and one charming and moving possibilities can float and float, like soft white clouds in a summer sky, —producing delicious effects of light and shade, but never precipitating themselves upon the sleepy land below in the positive, and often inconvenient, form of rain.

Among the distractions and annoyances of his parish work, during the constant struggle to communicate to his somewhat supine brother clergy a touch of his own superabundant enthusiasm, Mr. Leeper was often visited by thoughts of Elizabeth. His state of mind may be regarded from two points of view during this period,—of this fact he was quite sensible himself, and, for some cause, it troubled him. The social and material advantages which a marriage with Elizabeth offered him seemed to sink more and more out of sight; while the attractive power of her beauty and charm of her manner waxed stronger and stronger. Memory played strange tricks upon Mr. Leeper. Little delicate flowers began to blossom in the rather neglected and arid region of his heart. He knew this, and it irritated him. Should he say that he was being tempted to fall away from the great work that he had proposed to himself,—was he indeed disposed to desert the Cause for love of one of the fair daughters of men? Or was he merely turning the more gentle and human side of his character, long hidden under hard deposits of ecclesiastical and social theory, towards the gracious sunlight? Mr. Leeper could not tell: but he knew that, for some strange reason, he would feel happier if he could be certain that he contemplated marriage in cold blood—if he could be sure that he wished to marry for the sake of the Cause rather than for the sake of the woman!

He was a really devout man. He believed that all his life was ordered for him. He depended very much on the leading of circumstances, not perceiving that circumstances, in the case of a strong nature, have a curious tendency to lead in the direction in which that nature desires to go. Mr. Leeper determined to wait, to give the matter time. He did not say—as Wharton said later in a somewhat analogous position—that "something would turn up;" he held that if it was to be, the way would be made clear by a higher power. So month after month had passed

by, till, at last, quite unexpectedly, Mr.
Leeper was offered a large parish in the
active crowded manufacturing district
which lies in the north of Midlandshire.

Two years before he would have clutched
at the offer, simply because it promised to
widen his sphere of action, to put him into
a prominent position, and give him an opportunity of testing the working capacity of
many of those theories which he so ardently
cherished. Now another thought influenced
him. He had waited patiently; this might
be the looked-for leading of circumstance.
He would have more to offer Elizabeth ;
her money and position would be more
than ever desirable for him ; and the
prospect of wide influence and of self-
devotion to a great practical good might
be somewhat of a bait with which to
tempt her. Alas, alas ! Mr. Leeper's eye
was no longer single. He clung to the
idea of a leading ; and yet he felt bitter
against himself. Was it possible that,

like the church of Ephesus, he had left his first love?

When the news of Mr. Leeper's preferment got abroad, poor Mrs. Harbage naturally made a last and desperate attempt to secure her eldest daughter's future. Mr. Harbage, like Curtius of old, was compelled to leap into the gulf, and to find out clearly what his brother clergyman's state of mind and intentions might be. Unfortunately Mr. Harbage's self-sacrifice was not crowned with the same success as that of the ancient Roman. Mr. Leeper intimated that such few affections as he was unwillingly sensible of possessing were altogether engaged elsewhere; and the gulf seemed to yawn, deeper and wider than ever, between the eldest Miss Harbage and matrimony.

Led by that vindictive instinct, which so often animates the heart of an affectionate mother when one of her children appears to be slighted, Mrs. Harbage immediately

did her best to discover who was commit-
ting the unparalleled atrocity of engrossing
Mr. Leeper's affections. The memory of
former disappointments naturally beset
her, and she instinctively fixed on Elizabeth Lorimer as the culprit. Mrs. Harbage loved to proclaim, if not her woes, at
least the sins of others, which might in
some measure be supposed to produce
those woes. And so the rumour concerning Mr. Leeper and Mrs. Lorimer was set
afloat, which eventually, as we have already
seen, reached Claybrooke Rectory, and
caused a very distinct amount of annoyance to its inmates.

Mr. Leeper could not actually contra-
dict the rumour ; nay, he was disposed
to accept it as a part of the expected
leading. He determined that,—as soon
as the necessary formalities, regarding the
leaving of his old parish and taking possession of his new one, had been accomplished,—he would go up to London and

see the young lady whose image, for the last twelve months, had haunted him so constantly.

But having once given in to the pleasing notion that he was intended eventually to try his fortune with Elizabeth, Mr. Leeper became absurdly anxious to see her as soon as possible. It was not without one or two struggles that he decided to postpone his visit till all business matters should be settled. Poor Mr. Leeper had been accustomed to obey his own commands unhesitatingly for a good number of years: but now his inclination seemed sadly disposed to rebel against his will. He was sensible of the rebellion, and it made him stern and imperious towards himself. Men of his nature seem almost to buy the right of being somewhat harsh to others, since they are so unsparing to themselves. Mr. Leeper did not love his neighbour with altogether apostolic fervour : but at times he abso-

lutely hated himself—which, perhaps, fail-
ing the first, was the next best thing he
could do.

It was on a soft dull afternoon towards the end of March, that Mr. Leeper
found himself, at last, waiting on Mrs.
Lorimer's doorstep,—one of those warm
enervating days when spring seems to
come upon upon us suddenly ; deceptive
days, tempting persons of a sanguine disposition to throw aside greatcoats, and
believe that winter is altogether past,—
followed too often, in our uncertain climate,
by disappointment for the hopeful in the
shape of weeks of black north-east wind.

London seemed very hot and stuffy after
the bracing air of Midlandshire. Mr. Leeper
was less vigorous than usual. The warm
day made him feel a little limp. He was
rather nervous too, and was aware that he
was not in exactly the right state, either
of mind or 'of body, for a great undertaking. He had not decided how much he

meant to say to Elizabeth Lorimer ; he hoped again that circumstances would point the way for him. Few men feel at their best with the possibility of a proposal hanging over them, and Mr. Leeper felt decidedly uncomfortable at this moment.

Mrs. Lorimer was at home—so Martha told him. That excellent woman was somewhat moved at his advent. It was pleasant to her to see a familiar face from the Claybrooke neighbourhood, even though the owner of it was not held very dear at Claybrooke Rectory itself. She conducted Mr. Leeper upstairs with a considerable show of satisfaction, and brought him word that Mrs. Lorimer was engaged just then, but would be with him shortly.

It must be remembered that Mr. Leeper had been living quietly in a not particularly enlightened part of the country, for some years, and had by no means kept pace with the times in the matter of house decoration ; therefore the appear-

ance of Mrs. Lorimer's drawing-room
struck him rather forcibly. The rich,
mysterious colours of the carpets and
hangings, the strange crowded pattern of
the wall-paper, the quaintly-shaped furniture, the dusky blue covers of the chairs,
the profusion of pretty, useless, unnecessary
odds and ends—all surprised him a little.
The room was filled with the delicious
sweetness of a couple of flame-coloured
azaleas, in full blossom, standing in large
pots in the windows. There was a sense
to him of unrestfulness, of too much
meaning, in all this subdued colour, in
this multitude of forms and patterns.
He was strongly aware of the charm of it
all : but it was bewildering to him in a
way. He almost recoiled from it.

Mr. Leeper was not quite himself this
afternoon. He was easily affected. The
room seemed to him a little dangerous,
and even more enervating, to the moral
and mental fibres, than the soft spring day

outside. He hated to be influenced. He liked to dominate his surroundings; and as he looked round this room, with its luxurious decorations and sweetly-scented atmosphere, he became sensible that there was a risk of his surroundings dominating him. Mr. Leeper had starved his senses on high moral grounds; his senses seemed inclined to take their revenge on him, this afternoon. The memory of Elizabeth Lorimer's beauty grew stronger and stronger within him; he longed more than ever to see her. Yet he felt angry with himself, angry with her, distrustful of the leading. It seemed to him that, like Samson of old, he was being beguiled; his strength and his vigour were in danger of being stolen, hopelessly, yet deliciously, away from him by the fair daughter of the Philistines. Mr. Leeper's forehead crumpled itself up into very hard lines; and his tall, angular, black figure looked singularly out of place amid the dim richness of Elizabeth Lorimer's drawing-room.

He stood lost in a rather unpleasant reverie, when the soft dragging sound of a woman's dress on the carpet caused him suddenly to look round. Elizabeth had come in through the other room, and was standing with one arm raised, pushing aside the heavy *portière*.

She was dressed in a long gown of black brocaded stuff. The material was soft, and hung in graceful folds as she stretched her hand up to draw back the curtain. She wore some handsome old lace, at her throat and wrists, of that delightfully harmonious shade of colour which inartistic persons are wont to say is the objectionable result of a want of good honest soap and water, —there are people, though, who in their adoration of cleanliness would wash the bloom off a peach before eating it, I believe! Elizabeth's brown hair was knotted low down at the back of her head, and curled a little about her forehead, lending a certain pretty tenderness to her face. Her appearance intensified the feelings with which Mr. Leeper was already troubled. She was certainly very beautiful. He enjoyed and yet almost regretted it.

All this, though long in the telling of it, occupied really but a few seconds of time. Elizabeth greeted her guest very graciously, while he, on his part, presented rather a disturbed and harassed countenance to her gaze.

"I did not know you were in London, Mr. Leeper," she said, smiling as she held out her hand to him.

"I have come up on business," he answered. "My stay is not likely to be a protracted one."

"Then it is all the more kind of you to take the trouble of coming to see me," said Elizabeth.

Mr. Leeper looked at her rather anxiously. It struck Elizabeth that there was an odd intensity and suggestion of suppressed excitement about his face and manner. It was a little uncomfortable. But probably it meant nothing—she had not seen him for a long time ; and meanwhile she had been living among people who were quite the reverse of intense. Mr. Leeper's visit was a matter of very secondary importance to Elizabeth. Her thoughts were much more occupied with the fact that she had made a disagreeable discovery regarding her banker's book, and that nothing had been heard or seen of Fred Wharton, since the day on which he had so abruptly left her.

"Won't you sit down?" she said, settling herself as she spoke in a low chair by the fireplace.

"I would rather stand, thank you," answered Mr. Leeper, with unnecessary precision.

Elizabeth felt a little bit bored. She leant back lazily in her chair, resting her

elbows on the two arms of it, and holding up one hand to shield her face from
the warmth of the smouldering fire. Mr.
Leeper could not help observing the fine
pose of her figure, and the graceful turn of
her head as it rested against the dull blue
chair-cover. He did not want to remark
these things : but they were too strong for
him, and he could not help it.

" I suppose everything is going on much
as usual at Lowcote," said Elizabeth, feeling
that she must find some subject of conversation.

" I believe so," answered Mr. Leeper
shortly.

" Why, are you not just come from
there ?" she asked.

Mr. Leeper saw light : he wanted to
talk about his prospects and his work ; he
fancied it would restore his equilibrium.

" No," he said, " I have left Lowcote,
Mrs. Lorimer. I have a much larger and
more interesting parish now. I was not

sorry to leave Lowcote, I never had enough
to do there."

"Ah no!" said Elizabeth. "I remember your telling me that. Where are you
living now?"

"I have got a parish in the north
of the county," he answered. "A manufacturing district is deeply interesting. I
have an extended sphere of work and, I
trust, of usefulness. The people, I think,
will be far more intelligent and respon-
sive than in a purely agricultural district.
Personally," added Mr. Leeper, drawing
himself up and looking more composed, and
consequently more pleasing, than he had
since Elizabeth entered the room, "personally, I feel deeply interested in, and very
hopeful respecting the work before me,
—but I shall want help."

"Oh! you are sure to find help," said
Elizabeth, smiling. She rather liked Mr.
Leeper when he became enthusiastic.

"You think so?" he asked quickly. "I

trust I may, Mrs. Lorimer, for I shall want it. It is no mere pastime that I am undertaking, but a work to call out and develop all a man's powers and energies."

"That you will like," she said. "I fancy you haven't any gift for being lazy and merely sitting still."

"The parish has been very much neglected," Mr. Leeper went on. He wanted to fortify and brace himself with the thought of his work. "I shall have to reorganise the whole of the parochial machinery—or rather to create it, for at present it can hardly be said to exist at all. I must raise money to build a mission-room. I want to establish a coffee-tavern with as little delay as possible, for I am afraid the drunkenness is terrible in the low-lying parts of the parish. And, finally, I must try to restore the church, and I must have bright hearty services which will be attractive to the people."

"You have plenty of work before you,"

said Elizabeth, smiling pleasantly. " I
wish you all success in your undertakings."

" Thank you, Mrs. Lorimer," answered
Mr. Leeper—then he paused a moment.
" I wish," he added, looking at her earnestly,
" that I could awaken a strong interest in
your mind regarding my parish."

" I am very much interested in all you
tell me," answered Elizabeth.

She felt that she ought to have a great
respect for Mr. Leeper and his work. He
certainly had higher aims, and devoted
himself much more consistently to the
good of his fellow-creatures, than any
one else whom she knew. But Elizabeth
was rather worried and rather dissatisfied.
She was quite unequal to getting up a
sudden enthusiasm for the improvement
of Mr. Leeper's manufacturing parish.
She felt wearied in face of his vigour and
energy.—She let the hand, with which she
had been shading her face from the fire,
fall languidly down on to the arm of the

chair.   The movement was a slight one,
but it arrested Mr. Leeper's attention.
Again it struck him how beautiful she was.
He felt he was being hurried forward, and
being compelled to speak more clearly
than he had purposed doing.

"I have a very special reason," he said,
"a very special reason for desiring to interest you in my future.   You may not,
perhaps, just now be able to estimate of
what deep and vital importance your con-
currence in my projects may be to me."

Elizabeth began to feel a little uncomfortable.   There was a curious mixture
of determination and entreaty about Mr.
Leeper's manner.

"On two occasions," he continued, "when
we have had some conversation together,
you have given me an impression that if
a life of—perhaps hard—but noble work
and high endeavour were offered to you
you would not reject it."

Elizabeth raised herself from her easy

position and sat straight up, looking at Mr. Leeper with very wide-open eyes.

Mr. Leeper had tried to set his ideas in order ; to think of the Cause ; to magnify his work : but as Elizabeth, surprised and lovely, looked up wonderingly at him, all the feelings, which had assaulted him when he first came into the room, rushed in upon him with redoubled force. Not coffee-taverns, or church restorations, or bright services, touched Mr. Leeper's thoughts of the future with delight and glory. Alas! not the Cause, but the woman, drew him on.

He turned suddenly away and walked hastily across the room. Then coming back, and standing before Elizabeth, his face pale and working with emotion, he said hoarsely—

" Will you marry me, Mrs. Lorimer ? "

" Good gracious, Mr. Leeper ! " cried Elizabeth, getting up quickly. She was amazed out of all common politeness by

this wholly unexpected proposal. " I beg
your pardon," she added, recovering herself rapidly ; " you must excuse me.
Your question has taken me so entirely
by surprise."

" I cannot help myself," he said almost
fiercely.

Then poor Mr. Leeper fell very low in
his own estimation ; he used the Cause as
a stalking-horse, and he knew that it was
ignoble.

" Think—pause—pray consider," he
said, stretching out his hand with a warning movement. " Do not refuse a call to a
noble work. Do not hastily put aside a
chance of greatly benefiting others. You
could do so much, Mrs. Lorimer. You
might be a blessing to hundreds of poor,
degraded, struggling creatures. With
your beauty, your talents, your position,
think of all that you might do. Surely,
surely, these considerations must move
you. Pray pause before you answer me."

There was something positively alarming in the desperate intensity of the man's manner, and in the earnestness of his words. Elizabeth felt that she was almost wicked in not pausing, at all events, as he asked her to. She stood with her hands clasped tightly together, trying to be quite calm, and to keep her eyes fixed steadily upon his face,—though her heart was beating so that she could not see him clearly.

"I have no desire to marry," she said, as quietly and distinctly as she could. "I have no intention of marrying—none. I am quite contented with my present circumstances. You must pardon my frankness; this is a matter in which the simple truth is best."

There was a pause.

The passions of anger and love have a good deal in common. Mr. Leeper felt himself filled with a perfect volcano of righteous indignation. He forgot Sam-

son ; he took leave of the broad humani-
ties of the Old Testament, and turned
as bitterly upon the beautiful woman
before him as St. Athanasius himself
might have turned upon some fair wanton
in Alexandria of old. The Fathers, we
know, did a good deal of scolding at
times.—He fancied that he was about to
smite with the sword of the Lord ; but,
alas! for the easiness of self-deception, he
really smote with no nobler weapon than
the stiletto of a disappointed lover.

"You reject it, then," he said bitterly ;
"reject all I offer you without a second
thought. You reject high aims, an earnest
life, a noble dedication of yourself to the
good of the Church and of your fellow-
creatures. It is a dangerous thing to do,
Mrs. Lorimer. A thing that can hardly
be done with perfect impunity. And
what do you reject it for?" he added,
looking contemptuously round the room.
"For this! for luxury, and idleness, and

curious furniture, and delicate hangings ; for what pleases the eye merely, and leaves the heart vain and empty. You care only to sit here at your ease,—like Dives of old, to fare sumptuously every day, while the beggar lies at your gate full of sores,—while hundreds of men and women live the lives and die the deaths of mere brutes, and you will not stretch out a finger to help them. Ah! it is you," he said, "and beautiful cold-hearted women like you, who are the ruin of our day! You take plain hard-working men captive, with your charm and your loveliness. You bewilder their eyes, you turn their minds from high purposes, you make them fall in their own self-respect, you bewitch and fascinate them, you play even at caring for their work, you pretend to sympathise with them ; and then, in the end, you reject them,—you send them away with their hearts no longer honest, with their self-respect shattered, with the

haunting knowledge that they are per-
jured in their own sight and in the sight
of God.   I have offered you a heroic life,
and you——"

"Stop, stop," cried Elizabeth haughtily.
She was too angry to reason, or protest,
or justify herself.   The very touch of
truth in Mr. Leeper's violent discourse,
where he called her life useless, vain, and
empty, made her all the more resentful
towards him.   "You forget yourself
strangely," she said.   "You have not the
faintest right to speak to me in this way.
And understand," she added, with a cruel
light in her eyes :—"understand, once and
for all, it is not so much your work
that I reject—I could easily, at moments
even gladly perhaps, give myself to that.
It is the condition with which it is offered
to me that I reject.   I absolutely reject
you."

For a moment they stood looking at
each other.   Mr. Leeper seemed to shrink ;

he seemed to fall together somehow. He despised himself—which was far more painful to him than hating himself. There was no one point in the whole of this interview that he could remember with satisfaction. He had deceived himself; he had been in the wrong from beginning to end; he had betrayed the Cause at first, and at last he had been almost insolent to this woman in her own house. His anger changed to shame. The nobler part of his nature asserted itself.

"I beg your pardon," he said simply. "I have made a great mistake."

And he turned away without another word and left her.

Mr. Leeper travelled back to North Midlandshire that night, a bitterly humiliated man. He was disappointed in his love, and that was bad enough, after his long waiting and thinking: but, worse still, he was disappointed in himself, for he had been both weak and unfaithful to what he held to be the highest good. Fortunately the care of some five or six thousand souls does not leave much time for brooding over any disaster, however great. Mr. Leeper flung himself into parish work with almost alarming vigour. He was a stern shepherd, and drove rather than led his flock into the ways of righteousness and temperance. He gained a reputation for determination, for dogmatism, for possessing, to a remarkable degree, the courage of his convictions. But though Mr. Leeper changed very little outwardly as time went on, he never quite, I fancy, forgot a certain enervating day late in March, a beautiful and scornful woman standing in a luxurious and strangely perfumed room, and teaching him a wholesome though unpleasant lesson respecting his own fallibility and short-comings.

CHAPTER VI.

" Vain is the effort to forget."

THERE is generally a lively feeling of satisfaction in the remembrance of having played a difficult game and won it. I am afraid this satisfaction is not wholly amiable, and arises less from the thought of one's own skill than from joy at the painful discomfiture of one's opponent. When poor Mr. Leeper admitted his mistake, and retired humbled and worsted from the scene of action, Elizabeth was conscious of a certain proud pleasure. She rejoiced in his humiliation. But when the first heat of her anger against him died down, and she had time to think the matter over quietly, she became more sensible of hav-

ing received, than of having administered,
a pretty sharp rebuke.

For the last eighteen months she had
been trying an experiment. By the re-
jection of various old elements in her life,
and the careful fusing and mingling various new ones, she hoped to manufacture
happiness. She anxiously watched the
crucible ; drew forth a little of its contents
now and then to test them ; added fresh
ingredients ; fanned her furnace fire into
a flame, to try what more heat would do,
and then let it smoulder and almost die
into white ashes, to see whether a lower
temperature would be more efficacious :
—but, though she waited and watched
with admirable patience and constancy,
the elements would not mingle somehow,
and melt into the harmonious glow
of true happiness. Elizabeth began to
distrust the results of her experiment.
She bent anxiously over her work, she
applied herself to it more diligently than

ever : but in her secret soul a wretched
suspicion grew, ever stronger and stronger,
that happiness can never be manufactured;
that though all the kingdoms of the world
and all the glory of them were passed
through the alembic, yet not enough happiness could be distilled from them to satisfy
the thirst of one frail human creature.

Mr. Leeper had come fearlessly into the
mysterious gloom of her laboratory ; and
had told her—almost brutally—that her
experiment would be a dead failure, and
that her working at it was so much mere
waste of time.   Elizabeth had driven him
out with flashing eyes and scornful words ;
yet the longer she thought over it, the more
she feared that he had spoken the truth.

Wharton's disappearance had disturbed
Elizabeth very much; more indeed than
she cared to own, even to herself.   She
was almost alarmed at discovering—now
that he was gone—what a large element
his society, his music, and pleasant con-

versation, had represented in her scheme of happiness. She was annoyed at feeling his absence so much, and rather over-played the part of entire indifference in consequence.

She had been restless and uncertain before, as Mrs. Frank Lorimer had not failed to note. These unpleasant symptoms were aggravated by Wharton's disappearance. Mrs. Frank observed them. They made her acutely uncomfortable. She asked herself, more than once, whether she had not made a fatal mistake. But she gave no hint to her husband or to the world, of the share she had had in producing the present aspect of affairs. Like the bad characters in the Psalms, Mrs. Frank Lorimer kept herself close, and like them hid much mental discomfort under a remarkably flourishing exterior.

Nor were these more subtle and subjective troubles the only ones which my poor Elizabeth had to struggle with at

this period.   There were others of a plain,
obvious, and material character which
caused her a good deal of anxiety.   During the last year and a half she had spent a
large sum of money.   Decorating a house,
after the sumptuous and fanciful manner
of the present day, necessitates a considerable outlay.   Then Elizabeth had expended
a good deal upon her clothes.   She had a
natural tendency towards surrounding herself with the best of everything.   Wharton
had advised her to be charming and please
her friends.   She was charming ; she was
more—she was, in a way, magnificent.
No doubt it is a most admirable thing to
be magnificent : but unfortunately it costs
a lot of money.   Certainly she had not
entertained much, so that the actual expenses of her housekeeping ought not to
have been great ; yet even in this depart-
ment a good deal more had been spent
than was actually necessary.   Elizabeth
had been rather worried for some time,

but by the end of March her financial
position was such, that she perceived some
very distinct change in her manner of
living to be absolutely indispensable.

Frank Lorimer was his brother's execu-
tor, and was by way of managing Elizabeth's affairs for her. But, in point of
fact, they had hardly ever mentioned
money matters to each other. Frank had
plenty of other things to do, and had
troubled himself very little about his
obligations in the matter ; and Elizabeth
always had a tendency to take her fate,
rather forcibly, into her own hands.

It is never agreeable to allow, even to
oneself, that one has been needlessly and
foolishly extravagant. Still less is it
agreeable to invite the criticism of another
person in the matter. Elizabeth put off
speaking to her brother-in-law as long as
possible, though she had great confidence
both in his ability and willingness to
help her : but at last she had to admit

that no other course was open to her.
Not caring to include Mrs. Frank in her
confidence—she had conceived a slight
distrust of her charming sister-in-law lately
—she wrote privately to Frank, enclosing
various necessary papers and statements,
and begging him to come the first evening
he was at liberty and deliver his verdict
on the situation.

Frank Lorimer was of a very reasonable
temperament. As a rule, he had not the
least inclination to quarrel with things as
they are : but he had often felt it hard
that the world had not been constituted
on some principle which would have ren-
dered it unnecessary for him ever to have
to say anything unpleasant to anybody.
You may call this inherent sweetness of
nature, or a lamentable want of moral
courage, as you please. The more delicate
virtues always run the risk of being included under the head of reprehensible
weakness of character. Any way, Frank

Lorimer found no righteous satisfaction in rebuking the erring brother. And rebuking the erring sister seemed to him, if possible, even more objectionable. He felt that Elizabeth had been very careless and extravagant: but he had not the smallest desire to tell her so. Consequently he arrived at her house, on the evening of the day following Mr. Leeper's stormy visit, with a sense upon him that he had a most ungracious duty to accomplish. He struggled to put off the evil moment of delivering his opinion on Elizabeth's expenses as long as possible, and took refuge in a little general conversation to begin with.

"I heard from Wharton this morning," he said, when their first greetings were over.

Frank stood with his back to the fire, in the attitude so natural to civilised man when he finds himself in the house of a near relation or intimate friend.

· "It was only a line. He's gone down to Oakhurst—says he is gone there on business. That is really a refreshingly untruthful statement as coming from him. Fred's capacity for business is of the most primitive and rudimentary description, you know. I don't somehow understand it," he added meditatively. "It seems to me he must have been very much put to it for an excuse before he would take refuge in talking of business, specially to me. I can't conceive why he's gone off just now. The country must be hideously chilly."

Elizabeth had been standing near him by the fire. As he spoke she moved away, and sitting down on a sofa near the window, began furling and unfurling a black and gold fan which hung at her side, with an appearance of considerable interest.

"Oh! business means drawings, I suppose," she answered, without looking up. "I daresay he's got some fresh orders,

There are always a lot of people staying
at Oakhurst.   He may have arranged
to meet Mrs. Ostler Westcott there.   He
began a drawing of her last season and
never finished it."

"Yes, I know," remarked Frank.   "Westcott offended him somehow, and he
wouldn't go on with it.   Westcott is
rather a vulgar creature, I admit."

Elizabeth put up her eyebrows slightly.

" Isn't he sufficiently punished in the
possession of such a universally attractive
wife, poor man ?" she said.

Frank shrugged his shoulders as apolo-
gising kindly for the shortcomings of the
whole house of Westcott.

" She told me," Elizabeth continued,
" one day, that she made it a rule always
to go into retreat in Lent.   I inquired
where, and she said, ' Oh! at Oakhurst ;'
so she's sure to be there now."

" Pleasant for Adolphus Carr," said
Frank, smiling.   " Complimentary to find

yourself and your house regarded in the light of a practical renunciation of the world."

Elizabeth did not answer.

" If Wharton's gone to draw, why can't he just say so, though ?" remarked Frank Lorimer after a moment's pause, contemplating the hearthrug with an air of mild suspicion. "I hate mysteries. Wharton used to be so charmingly unmysterious : but he's changed somehow lately. He is preoccupied. Sometimes he seems as if he had something on his mind. It is a great pity. It will be very depressing if Fred follows the multitude to do evil and becomes serious."

Elizabeth bent down over her fan, and diligently disentangled the silk threads of the tassel of it.

" Don't agitate yourself about him, Frank," she said. " Mrs. Ostler Westcott may be trusted to restore anybody to a most becoming state of frivolity."

Frank raised his eyes slowly from the hearthrug and looked at Elizabeth with a sensation of slight surprise. There was a suggestion of personal feeling in her way of speaking which he could not help remarking. He knew that most pretty women have a disposition to dislike each other: but he had fancied that Elizabeth was above that sort of thing. He was quite willing to admit that she was often too emotional, and even a little exaggerated: but he had never supposed her capable of small meannesses or social jealousies. Both her faults and her virtues were on the grand scale, he thought.

Elizabeth made a graceful picture, in the softly-shaded light of her quaint room, as she bent over the tassel of her fan, with a pretty show of industry in the disentangling of it. As he looked at her, Frank thought: "She, at least, need not much fear comparison with any woman as far as beauty goes."

Frank had almost forgotten his unpleasant after-dinner conversation with
his wife on the subject of Elizabeth and
Wharton. It had taken place nearly three
weeks before, and Frank made it a rule
to forget unpleasant things as soon as
possible.

Suddenly, as he stood looking at his
sister-in-law, he remembered his wife's
suggestion. What so natural as that Fred
Wharton should fall in love with this
charming woman? And—for Wharton
was a delightful fellow—what so probable
as that Elizabeth should in some degree
return his affection?—Yet the notion was
distinctly displeasing to Frank somehow.
He quite acknowledged that it would be
absurd to expect every young lady, who
might have the misfortune to lose her
husband at one-and-twenty, never to contemplate marrying again. It would be
altogether too much to demand that all
young widows should devote themselves

to some such mild form of suttee.   Other
men's widows, he thought, might do what
they pleased:—but for Robert Lorimer's
widow to be thinking of a second marriage
within little more than two years of her
husband's death!—no, most decidedly
Frank did not like it.   He was conscious
of a sudden jealous tenderness for his
brother's memory.   How Robert had worshipped Elizabeth, and yet she hardly ever
even referred to him!

It often happens that when two people
are together who know each other in-
timately, without any ostensible cause or
spoken word, they will both fall into
the same train of thought at the same
moment.   You may put this singular
phenomenon down to mere coincidence,—
which, like charity, has a capacity for cover-
ing a multitude of inconvenient facts,—
or you may talk learnedly of brain waves,
and subtle magnetic correspondences between kindred minds.   The phenomenon

remains, whatever may be the explanation of it. Mr. Leeper's somewhat ferocious proposal of the day before had pressed the possibility of a second marriage clearly upon Elizabeth's mind. She had heard some slight rumours of the gossip regarding herself and Wharton, which had been going the rounds among her friends and acquaintances : but Elizabeth, confident in the honesty of her own friendship, had put it aside as a disagreeable impertinence, upon which she would not condescend to bestow a second thought.

Now, as she played with her black-and-gold fan, while Frank Lorimer stood meditating on the hearthrug, she had a sudden illumination. People thought that under cover of friendship she was trying to make Wharton marry her. Wharton himself thought so, and had therefore discreetly retired. Everybody— possibly even Fanny and Frank—thought that, to use a vulgar expression, she had

been throwing herself at this young gentleman's head!

Elizabeth sat aghast as this odious notion unfolded itself before her. Ashamed,
angry, and outraged, she looked up suddenly at Frank, dreading to read a con-
firmation of her fears in his expression.

Frank Lorimer was feeling somewhat
angry, too. He liked his friend immensely : but just at this moment he
was chiefly sensible of a keen feeling of
loving jealousy for his brother.

When Elizabeth glanced up, their eyes
met. Both she and her companion were
conscious of a curious sensation. All the
vague amiability had died out of Frank
Lorimer's face,—in as far as it was possible for him to look severe, he looked
so at this moment. This change of
expression developed the latent likeness
between him and Robert Lorimer very
clearly. For an instant it seemed to
Elizabeth that her dead husband was

looking down earnestly, almost reproach-
fully, at her. She drew back with a
start, and put up one hand almost as
though she wanted to force him away
from her.

The action was so rapid that Frank
Lorimer hardly observed it. He turned
away, and after a moment said quietly :

" Have you got that sketch, Elizabeth,—
I've often meant to ask you and haven't
quite liked to, somehow,—that Adolphus
Carr once did of Robert? Have you
got it, or have I ?"

Elizabeth straightened herself up and
clasped her hands tightly together in her
lap. Her forehead contracted sharply, as
with a sensation of sudden pain. . There
was a moment's pause, and then she
answered in a voice which she evidently
had a difficulty in keeping steady.

" I have got it. But—but why do you
ask just now ? "

" Oh ! I don't know," said Frank, feeling a little confused. "It occurred to me just now. I shouldn't like it to be lost, you know, and I couldn't find it. Fanny said you had it."

"Yes, I have got it," Elizabeth repeated. "Fanny was quite right."

Frank Lorimer's indignation was not of the burning order. Already he began to accuse himself of having treated his fair sister-in-law with a singular absence of the delicate consideration which was her due.

"Fanny generally is right, you know," he said, with a slight smile, wishing to pass the matter off as lightly as possible. Mentally he called himself an awkward brute.

Elizabeth had risen from her seat. She stood for a moment looking straight in front of her. Then she threw back her head with a certain defiant movement, and turning to her companion, said coldly:

"If we are going to talk business,

hadn't we better begin at once? I am
not quick at figures; it will take me a
long time to understand, I daresay. Shall
we come into the other room and begin?"

Frank Lorimer felt rather humble as
he followed Elizabeth into the back drawing-room. He told himself that he had
given way to a nasty suspicious state of
mind, and that he ought to be ashamed
of himself.—No doubt the sketch was
hanging up in Elizabeth's bedroom with
fresh flowers before it. Nice women are
given to arranging dainty little altars and
shrines, at which to worship their dead
saints. Frank felt very apologetic. He
had trodden on sacred ground without
making any decent attempt to remove
his shoes first. He felt that he had
given Elizabeth cause to be angry with
him. He was less inclined than ever to
say unpleasant things to her about her
extravagant expenditure.

"I blame myself very much in these

business matters of yours, Elizabeth," he said. "I'm afraid I have been wretchedly negligent. I ought to have looked after things more, and then you wouldn't have all this worry."

Elizabeth sat down at the writing-table, and began arranging the papers. She was vividly conscious all the while that the drawing of her dead husband lay, face downwards, in the drawer, just under her hand. She had squandered Robert's money to help her to forget Robert. The thought was hardly a soothing one just now.

"I don't think I need bother you with a statement of everything," Frank went on. "If you'll just agree to my suggestion, and leave the rest to me, I'll set it all straight."

Elizabeth looked up quickly, with a keenly-distressed expression.

"Oh no, no!" she said. "I can't let you do that."

"I don't mean settle it in the positive and material form," answered Frank, smiling. "It can all be arranged without any more trouble to me than the writing of a few letters."

"It is a miserable business," cried Elizabeth, getting up suddenly and turning away, while the hot tears came into her eyes.

"Pray don't make yourself so unhappy, Elizabeth," said Frank quickly. "Nothing so very desperate has happened, after all. You're in a little mess, but you're by no means bankrupt yet."

Elizabeth was always disposed to feel too strongly, Frank knew. He was prepared for that : but still the expression of her face did seem to him most unnecessarily tragic at this moment.

"What shall I do?" asked she, without looking at him.

"Well," he answered, "if you didn't mind going away for a time, and letting

the house for the season,—it's so pretty
that you might ask a fancy price for it
—I think we could put all your affairs
straight."

"I am quite willing to go," said Elizabeth. The house and all connected with
it represented so much annoyance and
disappointment just now, that she was
disposed to welcome almost any change.

"I suppose you could go down to Mr.
Mainwaring's, at Claybrooke, for the summer, couldn't you?" Frank added.

"Oh no, please! not there," said Elizabeth quickly.

She shrank from the idea of Claybrooke
under these circumstances. Elizabeth had
begun to feel that she had not behaved altogether nicely to the Mainwarings. She
recoiled from the notion of making use
of those persons whom she had formerly
neglected.

"Mightn't I go abroad?" she said. "I
suppose I should have to take Martha

with me, but I could live very cheaply.
I could easily find a quiet inexpensive
pension at Vevey, or somewhere about
there."

"Wouldn't you be awfully bored, though?"
observed Frank.

"Oh no," she answered. "I think I
should rather enjoy being alone."

At this moment, with the thought of
Fred Wharton's possible interpretation of
her conduct strong in her mind, and the
memory of her husband so strangely and
suddenly forced upon her remembrance,
Elizabeth had a sort of sullen longing
to escape from everybody.

"There are always the mountains and
the lake to fall back upon," she added.

Frank made a rather expressive face.

"I don't go in very much for mountains
myself, you know," he said. "They are
rather grisly companions when one is
alone. But you do just as you like,
Elizabeth."

"I don't feel as if it mattered very much where I went, or what I did," said Elizabeth, with a sudden bitterness. "I am afraid I am altogether a superfluity. Everything seems to go wrong with me."

Frank, not having the keys to the position, could only smooth his fair beard and wish, in silence, that women were not so much given to making general statements of a lugubrious and unreasonable nature.

After a minute he observed, in tones intended to be encouraging :—

"Fanny's bent on going abroad again this year, so I suppose we shall go. Fanny generally has her own way in the end. She and the children might join you in July, and I would follow as soon as I can escape from that everlasting paper."

Elizabeth did not offer any comment.

"Very well, then," he said, "you'll leave all these accounts and things in my hands. I'll see about letting the house at once.

We ought to let it from the beginning of
May.   Can you pack up and clear out by
then, do you think ?"

"Oh yes!" she replied wearily.   "I
can be ready any time.   The sooner the
better, as far as I am concerned."

CHAPTER VII.

"For a pinte of hony thou shalt here likely find a gallon of gaul, for a dram of pleasure a pound of pain, for an inch of mirth an ell of mone ; as Ivie doth an Oke, these miseries encompass our life."

IT is not necessary to follow Elizabeth through the fatiguing processes of packing up, arranging her house, and taking leave of her acquaintances,—many of whom were a good deal interested by the news of her approaching departure. Wharton not to be found, and Mrs. Lorimer letting her house and going abroad!—it looked very much as if something had happened. A good many questions were put to Fanny Lorimer : but the anxious inquirers were not very fully satisfied by her answers. Fanny Lorimer had private reasons for desiring to keep her own counsel ; and displayed a considerable amount of the ingenuity that her husband so much admired, in baffling her too curious interlocutors. Suffice it to say, that the house was let at a high rent to a clean and childless tenant; and that Elizabeth saw that her pecuniary difficulties were in a fair way to be eventually settled.

There is something depressing in the ending of almost any episode in one's career. The episode, in itself, may not have been very brilliant or satisfactory; yet there is a sense of regret as one turns the page, and says to oneself:— "This is done with, any way. It may influence the future a little, possibly: but, practically, it is past and over, and will never be read through again." So felt Elizabeth the last few days she spent in London.

Things seemed to have broken off short, and the future looked very blank and empty to her. In three days she would start on her journey; and she began to fear, with Frank, that the mountains might prove rather cold and unresponsive company after all. She had been packing and arranging and saying good-bye all day long; about half-past five a necessity for air and quiet came over her, and wrapping herself in a long fur-trimmed over-jacket—for the April evenings were still cold—she went out to refresh herself with a solitary walk by the river. She had been hurried and bothered in the last few weeks. She had been called on suddenly to form new plans, and take an entirely new departure. She wanted a little time to arrange her ideas and get some general view of the situation

There had been a good deal of rain earlier in the day, and the sky was covered with a layer of dull gray cloud. The rain was over, but the pavements were still wet, and the unlovely image of the lamp-posts was repeated in ugly zigzag lines on their shiny surface. The river was very full, and swirled by with little hurrying circles and eddies, here and there, breaking the face of its otherwise smooth and oily current. It choked and gurgled around the piers of the bridges, and then swept on again swiftly, reflecting the sad, coloured leaden sky above in its broad unrestful bosom. The buildings on either bank loomed, black and mysterious, through the dense misty atmosphere. The Embankment itself was quiet and deserted enough : but Elizabeth could hear distinctly, in the distance, the hoarse murmur rising up from the crowded streets. Suddenly a train rushed out across the railway-bridge, with a clang of metal and roar of steam ; and when the noise of it had died away far down in the south, she noted the sharp rattle of a hansom over a stone crossing, the steady thud of the horse's hoofs and the crunching of the roadway under the wheels as it passed

her,—another rattle over the stones again
in the distance, and the sound of it, too,
died away in the unceasing murmur of the
great, dim, toiling city.

A sense of almost intolerable loneliness
came over Elizabeth. There was something weird and strange to-day in the
hurrying river and in all these familiar
sounds. She seemed to be standing on
the edge of a vast world of movement, of
life, of earnest striving and endeavour, in
which she had neither lot nor part. The
past had not satisfied her hungry craving
for happiness, and the future seemed to
offer even less than' the past. Love and
marriage?—alas! she had tried them, they
were over, and had yielded but scant
delight. Friendship? — her friend had
grown tired, and left her without a word!
Duty?—Elizabeth shrank from the idea
of duty, it meant humiliation and self-
abasement. Mrs. Mainwaring's face, thin
and faded, came before her, and Mr.

Leeper's hot denunciations sounded in her ears.

While the wet south wind swept across the river, bringing the delicate flush of youth and health to her cheeks, and men and women, passing by, turned to look once again at the richly-dressed, stately, young lady pacing slowly along in the damp and dusky evening, Elizabeth felt herself utterly weary and desolate. Was it true, then, that life had little enough to give, after all? Did it really offer nothing but illusion, disappointment, hopes unfulfilled, solemn vows broken, fair promises forgotten? And then the end of it, cold, dark, and ugly; sweet lips that would kiss, kind hands that would clasp no more for ever; beautiful limbs lying rigid in death; eyes closed, and gentle voices hushed in everlasting silence; and beyond—a hope merely, a possibility,—to faith a promise, a pledge, but faith, alas! is often too weak to grasp it.

Elizabeth thought of the quiet room, shaded from the fierce glare of the southern sun, in which Robert Lorimer had panted his life slowly and painfully away two short years before; of the last smile with which he had turned to Frank and her as they watched together by his bedside; of the horrible chill and bewilderment that had overtaken her, when she realised that he would never move or speak to her again. Was it possible that this was all that life could give her, after all?

Elizabeth was filled with an immense self-pity. Those pagan instincts which are strong in every nature that is capable of being deeply moved by outward nature, by beauty, by the glory of physical health and physical joy, stirred within her. She revolted passionately against things as they are; against cold and relentless fact; against the sorrowful ordering of this world; against the strange unimportance of individual suffering in the general movement of things. It all seemed cruel, cruel, cruel. Why was she unsatisfied? why was she tormented thus? She rebelled against her fate; and, like Job of old, was tempted to " curse God and die."

Down in the west, above the jagged line of house-roofs and chimneys on the river-bank, the clouds were slowly breaking; and, between the long level lines of them there showed a space of open sky, —pale clear green, glowing into delicate saffron light down towards the horizon. It seemed infinitely far, ineffably pure, utterly peaceful;—set there for a token of final and everlasting rest to the troubled and struggling children of men. To Elizabeth it seemed to image forth the pale passionless rapture of saints and angels. It was of the heaven heavenly, she was of the earth earthy. She trembled and shrank away from the lofty purity of the Christian ideal, and demanded some more

immediate and material description of satisfaction and happiness. She was, she felt,
too much rooted and grounded in what
was simply human to be able to fling
herself for comfort on what was divine.
It seemed to her that the awful and
majestic figures of saints and martyrs,
crowned now with the undying glories of
their past sacrifice, and joyful in untiring
adoration, could never have been men
and women of like passions with herself.
They seemed useless to her for comfort,
or encouragement, or example. Their past
anguish and their present bliss seemed as
far removed from her ordinary, vain, and
trivial life, as the unutterable purity of the
western sky was removed from the muddy
swirling river, with its floating bits of wreck
and weed. Deep down in the river-current,
too, she feared, worse things than mere
broken wreck and weed moved sullenly
along,—foul dead things which had once
shown fair and graceful enough in the

genial sunshine : but now, for very shame, hid their dreadful and misshapen forms in the cold heart of the hurrying stream. So different, it seemed to her, were the human and the divine. The first had failed her, and she was desolate : but she had neither the faith nor the courage yet to repent, and throw herself unreservedly for comfort and support upon the second.

It was growing dusk. The long lines of lamps flickered along the roadway, while the still wet pavement gave back their blurred and distorted reflection. More than one passer-by had paused a moment, to look rather curiously at the tall young lady oitering in the chilly evening air. Elizabeth had been too busy with her own thoughts to heed them: but she was sensible, at last, that some man passed her and then stopped and turned back. Moved by a sudden impulse, she turned round too and faced him. It was Fred Wharton.

"Ah !" she cried, stretching out her

hands towards him. " I am so glad, so very glad you have come back."

Wharton, during his retirement in Sussex, had pictured to himself, pretty often, how he would meet Elizabeth again, and what he would say to her : but this meeting was both unexpected in itself and unusual in its surroundings. Between the weird spiritual light of the western sky and the uncertain glimmering of the vulgar gas-lamps, it seemed to him that her face looked strangely white and scared, her sweet mouth tremulous, her beautiful eyes wild. She looked to him like some lovely lost child. He could not stop to indulge in the usual little courtesies of recognition ; he longed supremely to protect and comfort her.

"Something is the matter. Somebody has frightened you," he said fiercely, possessed with a strong desire to find that obnoxious somebody and destroy the creature on the spot.

"No," said Elizabeth, "nothing is the
matter, and that, in a way, is the worst of
it. I have only frightened myself with
my own fancies. Ah!" she added, putting out her hands with a weary despairing gesture, "it is all too big for me."

A good-looking young man and an
unusually handsome well-dressed woman,
standing and talking earnestly together in
the twilight, are pretty sure to attract
attention and suggest interesting but
somewhat peculiar comments. Just as
Elizabeth spoke two men passed, and
Wharton heard one of them laugh, as he
moved away, and make some observation
to his companion. Immediately Mrs.
Frank Lorimer and all the outraged
social proprieties rushed into his mind.

"Hadn't we better walk on, Mrs Lorimer?" he said hastily. "I'm afraid it
may look a little odd for us to be standing here, so."

The observation jarred unpleasantly

upon Elizabeth. It seemed so cold and unsympathetic. When Wharton suddenly appeared before her in the midst of her loneliness and distress, she had turned to him with a sense of comfort and security. She had come nearer changing friendship into a tenderer feeling than at any previous moment of their acquaintance. Now his words almost seemed to imply that she had gone too far. She remembered her fears regarding the cause of his disappearance ; she recalled the gossip which, she knew, had gone about concerning their connection. Elizabeth's pride came to her rescue. She entirely recovered her self-possession, and turning, walked rapidly towards home.

" I am glad to see you, Mr. Wharton," she said after a minute or two, with a certain coldness and dignity of manner ; —" because I am going abroad the day after to-morrow. I shall probably be away all the summer. We have seen a good deal of each other, you know, at different times ; and I am glad to have this opportunity of saying good-bye to you."

Wharton observed the change of tone. Mentally he cursed Mrs. Frank Lorimer. He was, also, immensely surprised at the information Elizabeth gave him. It would simplify matters for her to go away, and yet somehow Wharton was conscious that he felt very sorry.

"But why are you going?" he asked, "This is so unexpected to me. Must you really go?"

"Oh yes, I must go," answered Elizabeth. "I have let my house for the season. I must go, and, indeed, I believe I should be very sorry not to go."

Wharton could not understand it. They walked on in silence for a minute or two, then he said rather inconsequently :—

"I brought you some white flowers the last time I was at your house,—that afternoon when you came in late.   I have wondered, once or twice since, whether you ever had them."

"Fanny Lorimer was holding them," answered Elizabeth, "when I came in.   She seemed to wish for them.   They were not really mine to give, but I let her keep them."

She walked on quickly.   She was anxious to get home as soon as possible, and not to prolong their *tête-à-tête* for a moment more than was actually necessary.   Just as they arrived at the house Elizabeth turned to her companion ; her expression was somewhat hard, all the gentleness had gone out of her face.

"You remember our compact?" she said.   "You have taught me something about friendship in the last eighteen months, and I thank you.   It has been interesting.   It is a very pretty game, only, unfortunately, it seems people so soon get tired of playing it."

Then she held out her hand to him.
" Good-bye, Mr. Wharton," she said.

Wharton ought to have been glad ;
things were certainly turning up ; it would
be very easy for him to accept the ruling
of events, and avoid further complications:
yet, so perverse is the heart of man, he
felt anything but satisfied.   In point of
fact, he felt rather desperate.

" But shan't I see you again ?   I must
see you again," he said.

" I shall be engaged all to-morrow,"
answered Elizabeth coldly.

" Not in the evening," said Wharton.
" Surely I may come in in the evening."

Elizabeth rang the door-bell.   She was
silent for a moment : but, just as Martha
opened the door from within, she turned
to Wharton and answered him quickly.

" Yes," she said, " you can come in in
the evening, if you want to."

Then she passed into the house.   On
the hall-table lay a gentleman's visiting-

card. Elizabeth picked it up languidly, and moved under the lamp to read it.

It bore a name she remembered very well—the name of Mr. Edward Dadley.

CHAPTER VIII.

" For auld lang syne."

As a traveller, lingering in the dusty glar-
ing streets of some far-off southern city
and hearing suddenly a few bars of an
old well-remembered tune, is carried back
in fancy, across land and sea, to the cool
English air and soft green English land-
scape, to home, and the simple vivid joys
and sorrows of childhood, to those clear
early days that seem to have no shadows
and no perspective; and, being thus carried
back in fancy, feels a sense of repose and
quiet and security stealing over his whole
being,—so Elizabeth, seeing Edward Dadley's name thus unexpectedly in the midst
of her loneliness, and confusion, and dis-

appointment, was filled with a certain
vague hope of rest and contentment.

It has been said, that first love is
infinite and has no second like to it. The
latter part of the proposition, I fancy, most
people will be willing enough to assent to,
whatever they may hold concerning the
first part of it. Assertions regarding
infinity are easier to make than to sustain,
as a rule. But first love has no second
like to it, for it is an initiation into the
mysteries, and must ever after exercise
a strange and subtle influence over the
mind. It is of the nature of a revela-
tion ; for the first time we worship in
the temple face to face with our divinity.
Many of us worship pretty freely in that
temple afterwards. We get to know
nearly every nook and corner of the building. We grow more or less accustomed to
the passionate strains of music and to the
rich odour of the incense ; we cease to be
much impressed by the " dim religious

light." Some of us even go further, and
discover that the golden image of the
goddess has feet of common clay ; that
the singers and musicians have a tendency
to gossip over the last bit of scandal, and
even to eat oranges, during the intervals
of the services ; and that the incense itself
may be bought extremely cheap in the
market-place just outside. Yet, notwithstanding the trying disillusionments which
come to us with time and knowledge, very
few of us can regard with entire indifference
the man or woman who first drew aside
for us the curtain that shrouds the temple
door ; who showed us for the first time the
eternal loveliness of the goddess ; and
taught us first how to move within that
mysterious inner circle of perception and
emotion which is commonly called love.

Elizabeth Lorimer's first lover—the
man who had, for good or evil, first drawn
aside the curtain for her—was a fresh-faced
young Englishman of a common enough

type. Clean-limbed, tender-hearted, willing to adore, and quite incapable of understanding the depth or the breadth of her character. He was not a very remarkable or admirable young man. He hunted, and fished, and made love, and talked rudimentary politics over a good bottle of claret after dinner, in a very commonplace way. He was not in the least troubled with ideas. Nay, further, when called upon by his father to do so, he had, after something of a struggle, followed the very sensible, if unromantic, example of Gibbon, the historian, and while he "sighed as a lover" had "obeyed as a son." Elizabeth's pride had revolted at his desertion of her; had revolted so strongly that it hurried her, as we have seen, into a marriage with Robert Lorimer. In a way, she might put down all the troubles of her young life to Edward Dadley's account; and yet—yet the memory of first love is very strong.

Coming in from her dreary walk on the
Embankment, parting half in anger from
her friend on the doorstep, Elizabeth
suffered a strange transition of feeling
when she found Edward Dadley's card on
the hall-table. She had not seen him for
four years. She did not know anything
about his present circumstances. She did
not even know whether he was married
or single : but she was filled with a longing to meet him once again ; to go back,
for a few hours at least, to that pleasant
easy time before she had known anything
practically of sorrow or disappointment.
She longed to breathe the morning air
again, after struggling in the heat and
confusion of the noon-day. Everything
seemed to be slipping away from her just
now. A foolish hope, a half-despairing
fancy, that somehow a meeting with her
old lover might make things clear and
straight, came over her. Elizabeth knew
dimly all the while that she was ignoring

the lessons of experience ; that she was fighting against fate; that she was refusing to acknowledge an inevitable conclusion. It may seem a little stupid of any person to do this ; and yet, to my mind, there is something wonderfully moving in the gallant hopeless determination with which the young fight against the hard teachings of fact and experience. They may be fools. They are fools, no doubt : but they are fools whom one suffers gladly, for love of their magnificent obstinacy and finely-tempered courage.

Elizabeth went slowly upstairs with the visiting-card still in her hand. She felt a little reckless—the world seemed, in a way, to be coming to an end the day after to-morrow. Meanwhile she would defy fate ; she would do what she liked ; she would give herself one last chance. She would see Edward Dadley somehow. And if nothing came of it ?—and in justice to poor Elizabeth, it must be owned that she had formed no clear idea as to what could possibly come of it—well then, she thought, bitterly enough, she would have to own herself beaten and let the world come to an end as soon as it pleased.

"At last!" said Mrs. Frank Lorimer in her clear emphatic voice as Elizabeth entered the drawing-room. "My dear Elizabeth, where in the name of patience have you been? I have been waiting here the most interminable length of time to see you."

Fanny Lorimer had a great power of letting plain uncompromising daylight into the minds of other people: but Elizabeth was too highly wrought—too entirely occupied with her own sensations,—to be awakened even by her sister-in-law's rapid and decided opening of the shutters, just at present.

"I have been walking, down by the river," she answered abstractedly.

"Dear me!" said Mrs. Frank, "doesn't

it strike you that it is just a little late for you to be out walking alone ?"

" I wasn't alone," observed Elizabeth simply.

" Oh ?" said Mrs. Frank, with a note of interrogation in her voice.

She looked rather hard at Elizabeth ; she had an impression that there was something odd about her. She wondered if anything could have happened.

" I met Mr. Wharton," said Elizabeth, with the same air of indifference and abstraction ; " and he walked back here with me."

A sudden cheerful alertness seemed to take possession of Fanny Lorimer's small person. Fred Wharton had come back, then, and just in time. She hardly knew how to be sufficiently thankful. She had not made a fatal mistake, after all. Elizabeth seemed strangely preoccupied : but that Mrs. Frank was charmed at — it certainly meant, she argued, that something had happened, or was just about to happen.   Everything was really going right, then.   She had hardly realised before how dreadfully anxious Fred Wharton's absence had made her.   Her present sense of relief was intensely exhilarating. She smiled a little to herself, and folded her small neat hands restfully on her lap as she said quietly :—

"You have an admirable indifference to public opinion, really, Elizabeth.   You know the circumstances and surroundings of your walk might strike some people as slightly peculiar."

If Fanny Lorimer had failed to awaken Elizabeth at first, she certainly succeeded in doing so very completely now.   Elizabeth turned towards her with a sense of considerable annoyance.

"What do you mean?" she asked quickly.

"Only that you are young and very good-looking," answered the other; "and that of course you run the risk of being talked about. You know everybody does that, unless they are immensely careful."

Elizabeth had not expected this sort of open attack. It seemed to her that Fanny Lorimer was playing exactly the same part that Mrs. Mainwaring had played two years before. It is interesting to observe how history repeats itself: but there are some experiences none of us desire particularly to go through twice, even for the sake of proving the truth of that valuable saying.

The drawing-room was warm after the cold damp air of the evening outside. Elizabeth felt both mentally and physically stifled. She had a sense of heat, and crowding, and confusion. No doubt her state of mind was exaggerated : but hers was a nature prone to exaggeration. Fanny Lorimer's words intensified all her distressing feelings. She felt as though she was caught in a great spider's web; the delicate, almost invisible threads clung about her, impeding her movement, almost choking her; wrapping her relentlessly and hopelessly round with their thin compelling strength. She struggled against this paralysing sensation; she determined angrily, come what might, to see Edward Dadley again.

"This room is intolerably hot," she said, for all answer to her sister-in-law's strictures upon her conduct.

"The fire is large," replied Fanny Lorimer calmly. "I suppose your maids are anxious to finish up your whole stock of coals before they go. Maids always regard incoming tenants as their natural enemies. They can't bear leaving a scrap of anything for their successors. I fancy we are all inclined to be a little prejudiced against our successors."

"The heat is intolerable," said Elizabeth again.

She moved across the room hastily

and threw one of the windows wide open,
letting in a rush of rain-laden westerly
wind, which made the heavy curtains flap
and the candles flicker.

"Oh! what a fearful draught!" cried
Mrs. Frank, putting up both hands to keep
a little of the unexpected blast from her
face. "For pity's sake, Elizabeth, shut
down that window, and come and speak
to me like a reasonable creature. If you
want to give me something, pray let it be
something more agreeable than a violent
cold in my head."

Elizabeth shut the window down
slowly. The cold air and the physical
exertion had done her good. She felt less
excited and bewildered, yet more determined than ever to have her own way,
in one matter, at least. She sat down
quietly, and looked at Edward Dadley's
card again. She observed that he had
scribbled the name of the hotel at which
he was staying in the corner of it.

"Now that the whirlwind has ceased," said Mrs. Frank, unbuttoning her long gloves with great composure, "I may as well tell you what I came here on purpose to say. Frank wants you to come over to dinner to-night. To-morrow he'll be busy all day. You really must come back with me this evening, Elizabeth. We'll have a lovely time putting the babies to bed before dinner. Now you'll please Frank and come, won't you?"

There was something soothing in the thought of those two small, prattling, curly-headed creatures in their little white night-gowns. They seemed to belong to the same simple unperplexed side of life as Edward Dadley. There was a sweet, though sad, expression on Elizabeth's face as she answered Fanny Lorimer.

"Yes," she said, "I'll come gladly,— especially to see the babies."

Mrs. Frank looked at her intently for a moment.

"You certainly are a very attractive woman, Elizabeth," she remarked. "There is a great deal of *cachet* about you. I enjoy immensely having you to think about, though I don't pretend to understand you. I hope you won't do anything very extraordinary while you are abroad. I should be so sorry not to be present if you do anything extraordinary. Pray keep it till the summer, till I come out to you."

Elizabeth always disliked these intimate reflections of her sister-in-law's.

"I suppose I shall see you to-morrow evening again," she said, ignoring Mrs. Frank's last remarks.

"Ah! my dear Elizabeth," rejoined the other, "that is really dreadful. Now I must confess all my sins. I ought to have done it before ; but something put it out of my head. I really have been a fearful

idiot,—I quite forgot it was your last day.
Will you ever forgive me?" she added
with a very bright smile and charming
little air of penitence. "It was horribly
stupid of me: but I made an engagement
for to-morrow evening."

"Then you won't be able to come
here?" inquired Elizabeth.

Fanny Lorimer's observations regarding
her walk with Fred Wharton had made
her acutely uncomfortable again. One of
the very last things she desired was to
spend an evening alone with him,—still
less did she want him to be third wheel
to the cart if Edward Dadley came, as she
intended that he should.

"Oh, we'll come in for half-an-hour,"
said Fanny Lorimer.

It struck her some arrangement might
be pending with Wharton. She did not
at all want him to be put off.

"Don't alter any plans for us. We'll
certainly come in. We haven't to go to

our affair till late ; and of course we should have come to say good-bye, any way. Now, Elizabeth, do come back with me at once," she added, getting up, " I'm sure you needn't change your gown. It is grand enough to receive the whole of the peerage in,—and Frank and I are very simple people, you know."

Elizabeth paused a moment before answering. She looked tired and pale, and yet her eyes were unusually bright.

"My dear creature, it will be long past the children's bed-time if you're not quick, said Fanny Lorimer a little impatiently.

"Oh, just give me two minutes," cried Elizabeth. "I must write a note ; I won't be long."

Mrs. Frank felt that things were serious. She was playing her game altogether in the dark. She felt that it was necessary to be cautious.

"I'll wait," she said. "But pray don't put anybody off on account of our engagement. We can quite well come in for a time to-morrow evening."

Elizabeth moved quickly into the other room and sat down at the writing-table. Fanny Lorimer waited, slowly buttoning up her gloves again. She was a good deal interested in the thought of Elizabeth's note. She felt very curious to know whether it would be addressed to Fred Wharton or not. She heard Elizabeth writing hurriedly for a minute or two. Then there was a pause, followed by the sound of paper being sharply torn up, and the fluttering noise of it as it fell into the paper basket. Mrs. Frank remembered those little sounds afterwards. She never quite understood why they had a special significance for her : but she never could hear them in a quiet room without thinking of Elizabeth's pale tired face and bright eyes, and of the damp gusty evening when she waited so long for her to come in from her walk by the river.

There was a sound of writing again. Then Elizabeth got up from her seat at the table.

"I'll be ready in five minutes, Fanny," she said as she went out of the room.

The adage says that there are more ways of killing a cat than by choking her with cream. There are more ways, certainly, of learning the destination of a letter than by asking the writer of it point-blank for whom it is intended.

Mrs. Frank Lorimer remembered that there was some delightfully quaint china on the mantel-shelf in the back drawing-room. She had often, she thought, wished to examine it. She strolled into the other room.—The china of course was the object in view, but she was obliged to pass close to the writing-table. On the open blotting-book lay Elizabeth's note. The candles were burning brightly, and Elizabeth's hand-writing was large and distinct. Mrs. Frank could not help seeing the address.

It surprised her very much. She had
never heard of Edward Dadley before in
her life. She had made almost sure that
Elizabeth was writing to Fred Wharton.
This little discovery put out all her cal-
culations ; yet perhaps it intensified the
interest of the situation. Fanny Lorimer
decided that she and Frank would certainly spend half an hour with Elizabeth
next evening.

CHAPTER IX.

"And sometimes, by still harder fate,
The lovers meet, but meet too late."

WHARTON passed anything but a comfortable day. He had a long sitting in the morning from the afore-mentioned Mrs. Ostler Westcott, a very pretty young woman who was just making a reputation in certain circles of society for her beauty. Generally Wharton enjoyed his work heartily, but to-day somehow he did not feel at all in the humour for it. He seemed quite unable to make satisfactory progress ; he was both irritable and pre-occupied, and gave his fair sitter some excuse for announcing later to her little court of friends, rivals, and admirers, that "Mr. Wharton was really rather a dull young man, and that she, for her part, considered both him and his drawings immensely overrated." In the afternoon Wharton, feeling that he must occupy himself somehow, decided to go out and make some calls : but, on second thoughts, he arrived at the melancholy conclusion that there were not any members of his acquaintance whom it would give him the smallest pleasure to see at this moment. Formerly he had very thoroughly enjoyed his own society : but times had changed sadly with him lately. He was beginning to find himself a very poor companion ; now and then he went so far, indeed, as to vote himself an intolerable bore.

When the time arrived for him to present himself at Mrs. Lorimer's, he felt as wretchedly uncertain and undecided as ever. The sudden outburst of strong feeling which had carried him away for a time, when he first met Elizabeth the night before, had died down again. He really could not tell the least now, whether he was in love with her or not. He fancied a certain feeling was there : but it wanted some striking circumstances to develop it and make it active. And how unlikely, thought Wharton dismally, were any striking circumstances to surround his meeting with Elizabeth this evening! The Frank Lorimers would be there. Everything would be just as usual. He would, most likely, play a little ; Elizabeth would probably be tired, and would not talk much. Then they would all say good-bye, and everything would go on just the same as ever. It was very annoying. Wharton had often laughed at his own peculiarities : but he had always done so in a very sympathetic spirit. He really cherished and respected all his oddities and little affectations. He thought himself pleasantly original. To-day he laughed at himself rather bitterly. There was a spice of contempt in his amusement. He was not sure that he was not a very poor creature, after all. Such a state of mind is far from exhilarating. Wharton knew that his evening-coat was faultless in fit, that his shirt was a miracle of ironing, that his collar was eminently the right thing, that he was in every way an unusually good-looking fellow ; yet, for all that, he was a thoroughly depressed and unhappy young gentleman as he walked into Elizabeth Lorimer's pretty drawing-room on this memorable evening.

Once inside the door, he stopped, utterly surprised and forgetful of his own little troubles, to contemplate his hostess,— over whom a remarkable change seemed to have come.

Elizabeth was standing in the middle of the room, with her head thrown back and a curiously intense expression on her face, as if she was listening for some ex-pected sound. In her hands she held a long rosary of large brown wooden beads, with a roughly carved crucifix hanging from it. She stood twisting the beads about in her fingers with a strange restless movement.

Elizabeth had come across the rosary that day—as she was looking over some drawers, in a cabinet in her bedroom. It had been put away there a long time before, and she had almost forgotten the fact of its existence : but, seeing it again, she remembered very clearly the circumstances under which it had come into her possession. Robert Lorimer had given it to her. She remembered, as if it were but yesterday, the sparkling beryl-green lake, the purple mountains sleeping in the still summer sunshine ; the gray walls of the monastery in the foreground, with trailing creepers, and delicate ferns, and great masses of crimson valerian, masking the rugged sternness of their masonry ; the laughing Savoyard boatman, in his blue shirt, with a bunch of red roses stuck in his rather dilapidated hat, lying lazily on his back in the long rank grass ; the quaint little booth just outside the monastery gate, where a gentle, patient-looking lay-brother, in sandals and a rough brown habit, set out his small wares—*bénitiers*, rosaries, strings of beads, little tin virgins, emblems of local and patron saints—to tempt the handsome young English couple who had just rowed across the glittering lake from the gay French watering-place on the other side ; while far away down in the south the rugged crest of the Mont Cenis, awful in its loneliness and the immaculate purity of its whiteness, rose up into the deep blue sky, blocking the way to the passion and the romance of lovely Italy. Elizabeth remembered the scene and the day clearly. It was one of those days that stand out from the experience of a lifetime—a day on which, it seemed to her, she had come very near grasping the phantom of hap-

piness which it had been her fate—or her
sin, poor child—so constantly and vainly
to pursue.

Now, in the hour of her need, she found
this rough wooden rosary again, and with
it she found a store of gracious and tender
memories.   A half-superstitious fancy that
it might help her in trouble, save her in
temptation, shield her from evil, came over
her ; and, with an unreasoning faith in its
protecting virtues, she brought it downstairs with her, and held it in her hands
when her guest came into the room.

But the rosary only attracted Wharton's
attention, when he first looked at her, from
the strange contrast it formed, with its
old-world suggestions of sorrow and pain
and penitence, to the rest of Elizabeth's
appearance.   She was dressed in a gown
of soft ivory-white cashmere, plentifully
trimmed with rich old lace.   The sleeves
of the dress were short, with falling ruffles
of lace, leaving her arms bare from the

elbow. The neck of it was open, with a
soft ruffle of lace around it too. On her
arms were gold bracelets, and round her
throat a gold chain with a square gold cross;
on her bosom was a bunch of deep-red hot-
house flowers, roses and crimson amaryllis.

There was nothing very extraordinary
about Elizabeth's dress, after all. Indeed
it was in a much simpler style than
that which she usually affected. It was
the change from black to white which
struck Wharton so forcibly. He thought
she looked younger and gentler, more of
a girl and less of a woman; while the
strangely pathetic quality of her beauty
seemed in a way intensified and deepened.
Wharton felt as if she could not be the
same woman that he had parted with, on
the damp doorstep, the night before. She
seemed changed altogether. He did not
know whether he quite liked the change
or not. There was a restless brilliance in
her eyes and a clear burning red in her

cheeks. As Wharton looked at her in her white dress, with the rosary in her hands, he had a strange sense that there was some terrible sacrifice about to be accomplished, and that this fair woman was the victim.

Elizabeth laid the rosary down quickly on the table, and then received him with a pretty show of cordiality. But it seemed to Wharton that there was a hint of coming disaster in her very brightness, which pained and perplexed him.

"I feel a little to-night," said Elizabeth, smiling as she held out her hand to him, "as if I was bidding my farewell to the stage. I am taking leave of my audience; I am going to retire into private life. I want to leave a good impression on the public mind,—for the public, on the whole, has been very kind to me. You see I have arrayed myself in dainty new garments, and filled my rooms with sweet spring flowers. You shall sing your good-bye song to-night, and then the curtain will come down, and the lights will be put out ; and,—I may be foolish,—but I have a presentiment, Mr. Wharton, that it will be altogether *adieu*, and not *au revoir*, to this poor player."

Elizabeth said the last few words softly, and with a touch of earnestness which was a little disagreeable to Wharton. He thought she seemed feverish and over-excited ; for once he became extremely practical and full of common sense.

" You've been doing too much, and you're tired, Mrs. Lorimer," he answered. " I've had dozens and dozens of presentiments which subsequent events proved to be entirely false, for one that has really come true."

Elizabeth looked down for a minute ; then she smiled at him rather defiantly.

" Very well, then," she said, " if you object to presentiments so much we'll forget all about them.   We'll pretend to be very cheerful and encouraging, and talk about the beauties of Switzerland, and the charms of foreign travel, and the relief of avoiding a season in London. I wish to be most accommodating, as I shall not probably see you again for a long while.—But I must honestly tell you that I don't think the country has quite agreed with you somehow. I fancy the March winds have blown away a good deal of your usual urbanity."

Decidedly Elizabeth Lorimer was not like herself to-night. Wharton looked at her curiously.

"Things have not gone quite so well with me lately as they usually do, Mrs. Lorimer," he said. "I have had a number of new experiences—interesting, no doubt, from one point of view, but not wholly agreeable all the same."

"That's a pity," answered Elizabeth quickly ; she seemed to have a sort of necessity for talking. "I don't think your

new experiences have quite suited you.
You have been working a little too hard
at them possibly. Your *cachet*, as Fanny
would say, is certainly to be serene."

"And I have been anything but serene,"
Wharton rejoined. "I have been dreadfully worried and bothered. I have been
utterly unphilosophic and——"

But there he stopped. Martha was
announcing somebody. Elizabeth made
a rapid movement towards the door, then
seemed to think better of it, and stood
still. Wharton looked sharply at her ;
her breath was coming quickly, and the
two spots of colour on her cheeks burned
brighter than ever.

Cause and effect often seem to a
bystander to be rather disproportionate.
Edward Dadley, as he entered the room,
certainly did not strike Wharton as a very
agitating individual. He was a tall well-
made man, of about eight-and-twenty, to
judge by his looks. Even in his even-

ing clothes there was a faint and distant suggestion of the stable about him, and his trousers undoubtedly were rather unnecessarily tight. A fresh complexion, bluish gray eyes, a fair moustache, and features calling for no particular comment—a kindly, trustworthy, unimaginative young gentleman, with a profound knowledge of horses and dogs, and sport in all its branches;—with a disposition, probably, to hold art, and books, and music in slight contempt, and to undervalue the more cultivated side of life generally : but still honest and loyal-hearted, and acknowledged universally in his own set to be a " thoroughly good fellow."

He came forward towards Elizabeth with a frank cheery smile.

" It's very kind of you to ask me to come and see you in this sort of way, Mrs. Lorimer," he said, shaking hands with her. " I was awfully sorry to miss you yesterday."

" I wished very much to see you again,'
answered Elizabeth.

Wharton stood watching her. He
fancied there was something constrained
and unnatural in her manner. She was
generally so composed, and almost stately,
in her bearing, that her present restlessness
struck him all the more forcibly.

" I am going abroad to-morrow, so that
I could not leave the matter to chance.
I thought you would forgive my short and
informal invitation."

Elizabeth said this prettily, looking up
at the tall young man before her. Wharton did not enjoy the situation in the least.

" I was only too delighted to come, I'm
sure," said Mr. Dadley very cordially.

Then he looked rather hard at Wharton.
He seemed to expect the latter to speak
to him.

Whether from nervousness or from some
subtle feeling of the incongruity of the
position, Elizabeth could not make up

her mind to introduce the two men to each other. There was an awkward pause. Dadley was the first to speak His voice was rather loud and noisy. Wharton noted the fact ; he was disposed to be observant of all this man's shortcomings.

" You always seem to be going abroad, Mrs. Lorimer," he said. " I called here about—well, let's see—last September two years I believe it was, just before I went to America. You know I've been to America ?" he added, with an air of simple importance which edified Wharton considerably.

" No," she said, " I didn't know it."

" Yes," Dadley went on, " I have though, Mrs. Lorimer. I had a very jolly time. A lot of sport. Everybody goes to the Rocky Mountains to shoot now, you know. It's quite the right thing. You've been, I suppose?" he added, turning suddenly, with an inquiring glance, to Wharton.

"No," he answered quite slowly, fixing his eyes meanwhile on Mr. Dadley's boots. "I don't shoot; and I always avoid doing the right thing on principle. It's a little—shall we say—unimaginative, to do the right thing."

Wharton looked up at Elizabeth as he said the last few words. There was something of surprise and disappointment in her expression; and she did not seem to hear what he was saying.

Mr. Dadley stared at the last speaker for a minute with an air of slight bewilderment. Then he seemed to conclude that Wharton had intended to be amusing, and laughed a little, in a civil perfunctory manner.

"But I was going to tell you, Mrs. Lorimer," he said, turning again to Elizabeth, "that when I called here before, you were abroad then. And they said something about illness, and I felt awfully sorry. I hope you weren't ill, Mrs. Lorimer?"

The colour died out of Elizabeth's cheeks.

" No, no," she said quickly.   " It was not I that was ill."

" I'm uncommonly glad of that," remarked Mr. Dadley.

He really looked quite relieved : but he continued to turn questioning glances upon Fred Wharton.   The young squire seemed to find something singularly perplexing in the aspect of Elizabeth's other guest.

Wharton felt nettled by this inspection. This man, he supposed, was some old friend of Mrs. Lorimer's ; possibly a distant cousin ;—perhaps they had played together when they both wore short frocks and pinafores—that thought was not wholly palatable to him.—But they were far enough apart now any way, and the man, whoever he was, had no right to presume upon his old acquaintance with Mrs. Lorimer.   His knowing her when she wore pinafores—if he had done so— by no means justified his staring, in that unmitigated sort of fashion, at her present friends.

Wharton moved away and sat down in an arm-chair by the fireplace—the same in which Elizabeth had sat when Mr. Leeper expended all the powers of his eloquence in trying to convert her to the Cause and into Mrs. Leeper. Wharton felt far from amiable; two are company and three are none. He had a very distinct feeling that he was the third just now. He began idly rearranging some tall white narcissus blossoms, that stood in a glass jar on a little table at his side. The flowers were very sweet. Elizabeth had filled all the vases and pots with them; and the air of the rooms was heavy and faint with their perfume. If he must needs be third, Wharton was determined at least to appear unconscious of representing that generally unwelcome member. But as he leaned back in the arm-chair, and, with half-closed eyes, watched his fair hostess and the tall young squire, his irritation grew stronger and stronger. Wharton was generally very respectful and tender towards all living things. The sight of a flower lying, fading in the hot dust of the street, among scraps of paper and rubbish, caused him actual pain. This evening he was possessed with a curiously vindictive feeling ; and, as he noted every word and motion of the white-robed Elizabeth and that objectionable young man, he pulled one or two narcissus blossoms to pieces, in the most wanton and hard-hearted fashion.

Elizabeth had moved across the room, and seated herself rather wearily in a chair on the other side of the fireplace, nearly opposite to Wharton.   Edward Dadley having discovered a solid and somewhat elevated seat, drew it up beside her and sat down too, giving the legs of his trousers a little hitch up just above the knee as he did so, and asking a number of questions regarding Claybrooke at the same time.

"That's an awfully nice old house of your uncle's, Mrs. Lorimer," he said. "I was wonderfully fond of Claybrooke, you know. I wanted my father not to sell that little place of poor Aunt Maria's, but he would do it. He's a capital fellow in his way—my father," added Mr. Dadley meditatively; "but I always have thought him awfully pigheaded."

Elizabeth smiled faintly.

"Yes, he is frightfully pigheaded," Dadley went on, with an air of strong conviction. "If he wants you to do a thing, he never leaves you alone till it's done. Isn't there something about a man bearing a yoke in his youth? Upon my word, Mrs. Lorimer, that's just what I've had to do. I've never had my own way yet about anything."

Edward Dadley leant a little towards Elizabeth, and looked full at her as he said this. Then he suddenly seemed to remember Wharton's presence again, and cast a sharp glance towards him.

Wharton happened to raise his eyes at the moment, and they met Mr. Dadley's. He felt singularly disagreeable. He gave an insolent little yawn and said slowly—

"I daresay it has been very good for you."

"It hasn't been pleasant any way," answered Dadley shortly, and turned to Elizabeth again.

"Have any of those Harbage girls married yet, Mrs. Lorimer?" he went on. "Poor old Harbage! I used to feel awfully sorry for him, you know. He really was a very good old sort : but Mrs. Harbage was an awful woman. It used to make me perfectly sick to see the way she crammed those wretched girls down every man's throat ; and poor old Harbage used to get so hot and miserable, and yet he always did exactly what she told him. That woman was a caution, you know."

Elizabeth smiled again.

"Everything goes on just the same

down there," she said. "People never seem to change at all in Midland-shire."

"I wonder if the waggonette with the canary-coloured body and wheels is going still," said Dadley, laughing. "It was the finest thing out to see poor old Harbage driving that waggonette, with Mrs. Harbage and all the little Harbages inside. Then do you remember that dance at the Adnitts' at Lowcote," he continued, throwing himself back in his chair, sticking his long legs straight out in front of him, and tucking his fingers into his trousers pockets. "What a nice dance that was. I don't believe I've ever enjoyed a ball so much since."

Edward Dadley paused and sighed, as if the memories of that ball were really almost too much for him.

Elizabeth was evidently trying to bestow all her attention upon her guest. She looked tired and pale : but she managed to keep up a certain show of interest in Mr. Dadley's numerous reminiscences.

Wharton, glancing across at her from his arm-chair, felt more irritable than ever. The conversation seemed to him in very poor taste. The young squire's vocabulary was lamentably small. Wharton thought him rather a coarse-grained person. It was unendurable to suppose that he should be in any way connected with Mrs. Lorimer's past life. Wharton pulled the head, quite savagely, off a narcissus flower, as if that was to blame in some mysterious way for his present annoyances.

" Do you remember," said Dadley again, turning towards Elizabeth :—" Do you remember, Mrs. Lorimer, the squire took a little too much of his own champagne at supper, and just as we were all going away, he seized on poor, dear, old Aunt Maria and dragged her out into the middle of the room, and said we'd have another Sir Roger ? 'Pon my word, you

know, I don't believe I ever laughed so
much in my life. Poor Aunt Maria was
in the most awful state. Ah ! that was a
good ball. Do you remember"—Wharton
began to loathe that phrase—" Charlie
Melvin wanted you to give him a second
valse, and you'd promised—all——"

Mr. Dadley checked himself suddenly,
and cleared his throat, with a rather un-
successful attempt at indifference, while
he looked quickly across at Wharton
again. It seemed to strike him suddenly
that he might be going a little too far.

Wharton had given over pulling the
unfortunate flowers to pieces, and had
picked up a book. He was not reading ;
he was watching his companions quietly ;
and wondering whether it would not be
much wiser and more dignified just to
get up and go. He was evidently not
wanted ; his position was a little ridiculous ;
and yet there was something about Elizabeth's appearance which made him very

anxious to stay. There was a strangely blank look on her face which he could not understand. If she had merely looked bored, he would have thought it natural enough under the circumstances : but she looked something more than bored. Wharton had a conviction that a good deal was going on around him that he could not fathom at present. Then, Mrs. Lorimer was going away to-morrow. He put his dignity in his pocket, and decided to remain.

" I've never been back to Claybrooke since," said Mr. Dadley, leaning towards Elizabeth slightly as he spoke. " I've not seen any of the people for years. But sometimes I think, do you know, Mrs. Lorimer, that I never enjoyed any time in my life so much as those two winters."

Elizabeth's face flushed slightly. She tried to smile : but the attempt was not a very successful one.

There was an uncomfortable silence.

Dadley got up, and stood with his hands behind him and his back to the mantelpiece—giving a little kick with each foot to settle his trousers down into their proper place over his knees. He cleared his throat again and looked at Wharton.

"London's uncommonly full for the time of year," he remarked.

"Oh—er—were you speaking to me?" asked Fred Wharton, putting up his eyebrows slightly and shutting his book. "Perhaps London is full," he added. "I really don't know. It's not a subject I have very carefully considered."

Edward Dadley contemplated the toes of his shoes for a moment:—it is remarkable how much inspiration a certain class of men seem to derive from the contemplation of their shoes. Then he looked at Elizabeth for a minute, rather regretfully. He was not an observant person: but he was aware that he and his companions were at sixes and sevens.

He was an honest-hearted fellow; he
believed that there was a mistake somewhere; he feared that he was putting his
hostess in a false position.   He gave a
little sigh, and then said—

"Well, I'm going to settle down at last,
Mrs. Lorimer.   You're such an old friend
that I should like you just to wish me good
luck, and all that sort of thing, you know."

He paused.

"I'm going to be married; I'm going
to marry my cousin.   She's a good little
girl; and ——" again Dadley paused.
"I'm sure," he went on, with a sort of
rush, "if you should be coming up north
any time, and would look us up, I'm sure
I—I mean she, my cousin, you know—
bother it—my wife and I should be only
too happy to see you, and," he added,
looking towards Wharton, with a civil
smile, "your husband——"

Elizabeth started up; she gave a low
cry, as if in actual pain.

"Husband?" she cried. "My husband? what do you mean?"

Edward Dadley stared at her in utter
amazement. He made a motion towards
Wharton.

"Why, Mr. Lorimer," he said.

Wharton had started up too, with a
smothered exclamation of a somewhat
violent order. Could anything be much
more disastrous, he thought, than to be
taken for the dead husband of the woman
you had more than half a mind to propose
to? He would have spoken: but he was
absolutely dominated by the strength and
power of Elizabeth's emotion.

She stood there, looking like some
beautiful wild creature, which, hopeless of
escape, turns, with an agony of despair
and entreaty in its eyes, upon its pursuers.

"Ah!" she cried again passionately.
"My husband? You don't know what
you have said. You don't know what
you have done. And yet I ought to

thank you, for you have shown me what I really am. My husband?" she stretched out both hands and then let them fall despairingly at her sides. "Ah! God help me!" she said.

There was a depth of sorrow in the tones ‚of her voice and in her gesture, which filled both men with pity. But Wharton, even in the midst of his pity, was sensible of the artistic beauty of her appearance. "What an effect on the stage," he thought. Dadley was simply and utterly distressed.

"God bless my soul," he said distractedly, "what have I done?"

Elizabeth could not control her voice sufficiently to answer. She looked at Wharton for a moment, and then turned away.

"Hush, hush," said Wharton, "haven't you heard?—don't you know?"

He glanced at Elizabeth. He had a horrible feeling that he was going to wound or maim her in some way: but there was no alternative.

"Mr. Lorimer died," he said very quietly and clearly, " two years ago, in the south of France."

"God bless my soul," said Edward Dadley again. " Nobody had told me. I didn't know it."

The tears came into his eyes. He felt he would have given five years off his life —which was certainly generous, for men of Edward Dadley's type distinctly prefer this world to the next—to have left those unfortunate words unsaid. His old love for Elizabeth had stirred very strongly within him this evening. He was bound in honour to the " good little girl " up in the North: but he told himself sadly that Mrs. Lorimer was the handsomest and most attractive woman he had ever known ; and he cursed the ill-luck which had prevented his hearing that she was free, till now, when he himself was bound.

CHAPTER X.

"I fain would follow love, if that could be ;
I needs must follow death, who calls for me."

THERE is but one step from the sublime to the ridiculous, and it is really a very great relief to take that step sometimes. So, at least, Fred Wharton felt, when, at this awkward and uncomfortable period of the evening, Mrs. Frank Lorimer rustled into the room. He had been anathematising her pretty freely in private during the last month or six weeks : but on this particular occasion he was disposed to hail her advent as that of a veritable angel of deliverance.

Mrs. Frank was in a state of the most refreshing self-complacency. She was wearing for the first time a new and

very elaborate gown that had arrived
from Paris the week before. She felt
wonderfully urbane, and equal to almost
any emergency. Her dress had a very
long train to it, which, when she walked
into the room and stopped suddenly in
front of her hostess, caused her husband
—who was following her closely—no
small inconvenience. He had to perform a series of rather undignified little
gymnastics in the background to avoid
falling over, or otherwise damaging, the
wilderness of lace and flounces which
barred his onward path.

"My dear Elizabeth, how fearfully ill
you look!" exclaimed Mrs. Frank.

She glanced curiously at Wharton and
Dadley as she spoke. She had not
counted on finding three persons all looking embarrassed and agitated. Two she
would not have minded finding in some
such condition, but three seemed to her
altogether one too many.

"What have you been doing?" she asked.

There was an imploring expression on Elizabeth's face which made her stop. Fanny Lorimer had plenty of tact when she chose to use it.

"I suppose it's that white gown which makes you so pale. You must pardon my saying so, Elizabeth, but you know white is trying if one's tired. And I dare-say you're dreadfully tired with all that wretched packing.—I'm so glad to see you again," she added, turning with a charming little air of innocent pleasure to Wharton. "We were beginning to be quite nervous about you. I wanted to apply to one of these offices, don't you know, which are advertised in the daily papers where they find missing friends for you and all that sort of thing. I hope you settled your business com-fortably before you left Sussex? We all felt so interested in it though we hadn't the ghost of a notion what it was."

"You are too kind, Mrs. Lorimer," said Wharton, bowing.

The angel of deliverance carried a small sword apparently—still, sword or no sword, she was welcome.

Frank had been too busy avoiding his wife's train to take in any general impression of the situation on first entering the room. He saw that there was a stranger present ; it seemed to him that both Elizabeth and Wharton were silent and constrained. Everybody looked rather odd and confused, he thought : but it really was no particular business of his. Frank contented himself with stroking his fair beard and wondering mildly whether anything could be the matter.

Elizabeth introduced Edward Dadley to her sister-in-law, and Mrs. Frank embarked immediately in a lively conversation. Mr. Dadley's powers in that line

were never very great, and at this moment
he was not a little disturbed, and was
consequently even below his average in
conversational ability. But Mrs. Frank
was so serenely self-satisfied, owing to her
Paris gown, that she would, I believe,
have been capable of carrying on a deeply
interesting conversation with a hydro-
cephalous idiot if necessary.

Seeing that Dadley was safely provided
for, Elizabeth moved across the room to
speak to Frank, who was engaged in
welcoming Wharton back to civilised life
again, and in making inquiries about
Adolphus Carr and his charming house in
Sussex. As Elizabeth came up Wharton
turned away. He could not quite recover
his ease of manner in her presence, after the
very false position in which Edward Dadley's unfortunate mistake had placed him.

"Mr. Wharton," said Elizabeth softly,
without looking at him, "will you do
me a kindness?—will you go and play?

It would be a relief, for I am too tired to talk."

There was something graceful in this appeal which touched Wharton. It meant, he thought, that she wished him to understand that she attached no blame to him for the distressing scene that had just taken place.

"Yes," he answered, quickly turning to her. He was shocked by the pallor and sadness of her face.

Wharton went away into the back drawing-room and, settling himself at the piano, began playing rather tumultuously the first thing that came into his head.

"I am afraid I can't talk, Frank," said Elizabeth, sitting down wearily by him. "I suppose I'm over-tired. My head aches distractingly."

Frank looked down at her kindly. Her appearance pained him. He wished he could take care of her and do her some little service in a quiet brotherly way.

"You're simply tired out," he said. "I don't half like your going off all alone to-morrow without any of us."

Elizabeth smiled faintly.

"I shall be better alone, I think," she answered.

There was a long silence between them. While Wharton went on playing,—slipping from one thing into another with pleasant readiness and ease ;—and while Mrs. Frank discoursed to Dadley, who became more and more filled with the conviction that he was in the presence of " an awfully clever woman,"— Elizabeth sat staring straight in front of her, with her hands lying clasped in her lap. She felt dazed and stricken. The world had come to an end, after all,—all she wanted now was to keep herself steady and calm till they had gone away, and she was left to herself. Wharton, playing on almost mechanically, wandered at last into the accompaniment of the song of love, and death, and parting, which Elizabeth had said he must sing to her earlier in the evening. He remembered himself immediately and changed the motive: but the air had struck Elizabeth at once. She recalled the words only too clearly. She tried hard to master herself. With a sort 'of desperate gasp she put up one hand and pushed the soft brown hair back from her forehead.

Frank noticed the movement. He did not know what was the matter with her: but he grew a little frightened. He thought she was going to cry, and of all things he hated to see a woman crying.

"We'd much better go and leave you quiet," he said. "You are regularly knocked up; and you'll have to go off by the seven o'clock express, I suppose, to-morrow."

"If you go, please take them with you," said Elizabeth, with a motion of her hand towards Dadley and Wharton.

Wharton was not so absorbed in his music but that he managed to see pretty clearly what was going forward in the other room. He saw Frank get up and go and speak to his wife, who turned to Elizabeth and talked to her with a good deal of vivacity for a minute or two,— apparently she was offering a lot of good advice regarding the next day's journey. Then the two women kissed each other with a pretty show of affection. Edward Dadley shook hands with Elizabeth and said something,—Wharton could not quite hear what, but he thought he recognised the word " awfully." Evidently they were all going away. Wharton played on, he hardly knew why.

When Frank had bidden Elizabeth good-bye he came over to the piano, and laid his hand on Wharton's shoulder.

" We're going, my dear fellow," he said, " and you must come too. She is quite knocked up, and I want her to be quiet."

Wharton got up with a hopeless feeling upon him. It was a wretched ending to a wretched evening. Everything had gone against him. He had had no chance.

He went up to Elizabeth.

" I suppose I must go too, Mrs. Lorimer ?" he said.

Elizabeth held out her hand to him. There was a blank look on her face. She tried to smile, but the smile died away again and she did not speak.

Wharton went out of the room feeling just a little mad ; he ran downstairs after Frank, and began putting on his coat with a considerable absence of his accustomed composure ; he wanted to get out of the house and be quit of it all.

" I knew Mrs. Lorimer years ago down at Claybrooke," Edward Dadley was saying to Mrs. Frank, while he helped her, with more gallantry than handiness, to wrap herself in her fur cloak.

Ah yes," she answered.

" She isn't a bit altered," added Dadley.

For some reason or other this observation infuriated Wharton. It made him feel wild. It seemed as if Elizabeth Lorimer was being claimed by this man.

Martha had just opened the door, and two cabs were waiting outside in the dimly-lighted street. The night was cold and chilly, with a drizzling rain.

Wharton came to a sudden desperate determination. He began taking off his overcoat again.

" I've forgotten something I must say to Mrs. Lorimer," he said, turning to Frank. " Don't wait for me. I'll follow you in five minutes."

" Oh, my dear fellow, don't go back now," answered Frank Lorimer quickly. " Do let her be quiet. She's tired to death."

" I won't be long," Wharton said again. " I must just speak five words to her."

Frank would have protested further, but his wife, who had watched this little

scene with lively feelings of interest, called
out to him rather impatiently :—

"For pity's sake, make haste, Frank.
You and Mr. Wharton will have plenty of
other opportunities for conversation. Pray
don't keep me meditating for ever on this
wet doorstep !"

Edward Dadley laughed his company
laugh.   He fancied Mr. Frank Lorimer
must get the worst of it sometimes.

Very reluctantly Frank followed his
wife, best gown and all, out to the cab.
The front door banged, the two cabs
rattled away in different directions, and
then Wharton made his way upstairs
again.   He had a feeling that his conduct was a little peculiar, that some people
might, not unjustly, accuse him of a want
of delicate feeling in going back thus
after having bid his hostess good-bye :
but Wharton had got to a point where he
cared very little what anybody might say
or think ; he only knew that there was an

absolute necessity upon him to see Elizabeth Lorimer again.

The door of the back drawing-room was standing half open on to the landing. Wharton waited a moment to steady himself. He was about to take the most important step he had ever taken in his life, and his old habit of looking calmly at the situation reasserted itself.

The house was very quiet. As he paused in the doorway he became aware of a low sound in the air,—a sound not very often heard in luxurious rooms amid warmth and beauty and the sweet scent of flowers, but a common enough sound, alas! for all that. Wharton associated it with dusky forms crouched down on doorsteps at night, half-seen by the passers-by in the dingy gaslight; or sad tattered figures, loitering aimlessly at street corners in the bleak mist and fog of dull gray evenings. It was only the sound of a woman sobbing; and that not loudly—

sobbing quietly, as though hope was dead and her own heart nearly broken.

Wharton waited a minute or two hoping that the sobbing would cease, but it did not do so. The sound became terrible,— a perfect nightmare,—to him. He could bear it no longer. He felt he ought to go away, and yet the desire to see Elizabeth once more grew stronger and stronger. He pushed the door wide open and went into the room.

Wharton had listened to the sound which arrested his attention as he paused in the doorway with considerable emotion : but it had hardly prepared him for the scene within.

Elizabeth had sunk down on to the floor, near the big arm-chair in which Wharton had sat so quietly nursing his resentment against the obnoxious young squire earlier in the evening. She was in a half-kneeling half-sitting position. She had thrown her bare arms out, with a passionate gesture, across the little black wooden table at her side. Her face was pressed down upon her two hands. The vase of narcissus flowers was overturned, and the pure white blossoms were scattered on the carpet.

Wharton's first instinct was to retire. He could hardly bring himself to look at the usually quiet stately Elizabeth as she lay there shaken with the storm of her grief. He had an idea that, except on the stage, a woman's emotions should be as carefully veiled as her form. It seemed to him almost sacrilegious to permit himself to see her now, when she had thrown aside all conventional restraint, and was laying bare her inmost heart in the wild abandon of her sorrow. Wharton had always cultivated a general spirit of benevolence, but he had had very little experience in the active art of consolation. So bewildered was he by the situation in which he found himself that he hardly

knew how to act. It seemed inhuman to
go away and leave her thus. He could
not do it. Yet if he stayed he was in
honour bound to let her know at once
that he was in the room.

" Mrs. Lorimer," he said gently. " Mrs.
Lorimer."

The pains of birth are cruel, even
more cruel perhaps than those of death.
With bitter pangs and burning tears a
new and nobler life was being born within
Elizabeth. She had seen her old lover
again, and his own words had, in a
strangely vivid way, recalled the image of
her husband. For a moment the two
men had seemed to stand side by side.
Elizabeth had compared them and judged
them, and then turned away sick at heart.
All her past had risen up before her.
The but half-hearted courtship and marriage ; her own sense of bewilderment
amid the new conditions of her life ; the
haunting thoughts of the boy-lover whom

she had cared for with innocent girlish fondness ; her husband's illness and death ; her rebellion against God and against sorrow ; her angry disdain of simple duty; her determination to over-live her trouble ; her restless desire for amusement, and her not wholly successful attempt at friendship,—all these things came to her remembrance and overwhelmed her.

She lay, in a very agony of contrition, with her face pressed down upon her hands,—in which she clutched the wooden rosary,—when Wharton's voice suddenly aroused her.

Elizabeth struggled up on to her feet. As she did so Wharton saw that her face was all marred and disfigured with crying. The flowers she wore were crushed and broken. They had made a great, dull, red stain upon the bosom of her white dress. There was something very hideous to Wharton in that stain. He could not take his eyes off it or forget it.

With a violent effort, Elizabeth controlled her sobs and turned upon him haughtily.

"Why are you here?" she said. "Why have you come back in this way, without any warning?"

Wharton admired the fine courage with which she tried to protect herself in her extremity. He felt at a dreadful disadvantage.

"Forgive me," he answered. "I could not help myself. I was obliged to come back. I have something I must say to you, and this is my only chance since you are going away to-morrow."

"You must leave me," said Elizabeth harshly, without looking at him. "I want to be alone."

But Wharton felt he had gone too far to turn back now.

"It is impossible for me to leave you in this condition," he said quietly. "As your friend, Mrs. Lorimer, I have a right to stay till you are calmer."

"It will do no good," Elizabeth answered bitterly. "You cannot help me; nobody can help me. I must bear my trouble alone. People don't die of grief, they say—or of repentance either, for that matter," she added.

"Still I shall stay," said Wharton.

A look of dead indifference settled down on Elizabeth's face. If he would stay, he must. After the first flash of womanly anger had died away, she did not really care very much whether he stayed or not. She was so absorbed in her own emotions that she was almost unconscious of the presence of another person. There was no trace of the coquette about Elizabeth. She did not pose: she simply felt.

She sat down in the arm-chair. Wharton stood waiting. For some time there was silence between them. At last he said:—

"Mrs. Lorimer, this is dreadful. You must tell me what has happened."

"I cannot tell you," she answered, speaking slowly and with some difficulty. "I cannot tell any one."

Then she added, after a minute or two :—"I have had a terrible experience to-night. Can you fancy what it is suddenly, in a moment, to be filled utterly with self-reproach? To have built yourself a fair dwelling-house, and in the time of your utmost need to find that it is built on the sand? To see it crack and crumble around you, to see it washed away for ever, while you stand homeless and desolate? Oh! Robert, Robert!" she cried, breaking suddenly into a wild passion of grief. "Oh! my darling, forgive me! I have tried to forget you. I have wanted to fling all the past behind me. I have wanted so desperately to be happy. You, who have entered into that perfect peace where all our miserable selfish desires and jealousies fade away, forgive me, pardon me!"

Elizabeth stood up. The flood-gates were open, and, utterly regardless of Wharton's presence, she poured forth her heart in speech.

" To-night," she went on, " I have learnt the truth. Too late I have seen my fatal mistake. I have looked back at my past life ; I see that I have missed the meaning of it all, and that self, self, nothing but self, is written across every page of it. I might have found fulness of joy in wedded love ; bitter-sweet joy in mourning ; calm and chastened joy in duty and obedience. I have rejected it all. Ah! believe me," she said, turning suddenly to him, " God is merciful. He forgives. Soiled and weary, but repentant, we may still creep into heaven at last. But He is terribly just. What we sow, that, and that only, can we reap. I have sowed to myself, and I reap the fruit of my sowing—sorrow, emptiness, a fearful sense of waste. Yet I cannot complain. It is bitter—no one else can ever know how bitter: but it is all my own doing, and it is only just."

. To Wharton there was something almost sublime in this submission. He thought of our Lady of Sorrow again; and could have kneeled down and worshipped the woman who stood before him, crowned with the glory and the anguish of her utter self-abasement.

After a little time she looked up again. All the hardness had melted out of her face, and there was something very wistful and tender in its expression.

"If I had only lived two or three hundred years ago," she said, "I should have gone away now and buried my mistakes and repentance in some convent. I should have put on coarse garments; have brought my body into subjection with fasting and penance; have hardened my hands with labour, and——"

"Don't," cried Wharton suddenly, with

a shudder. "Pray don't, Mrs. Lorimer. I can't stand this."

Elizabeth smiled faintly, but her lips were tremulous.

"Why not?" she asked gently. "I think, do you know, I could be very peaceful and contented in some quiet place, where high walls shut out the world, and where I might tend poor, old, sick folk and teach little children. But this is a mere fanciful dream, touched with self-love again—I can't do this."

"No, thank God, you can't," he said under his breath.

"I must do something, in a way, far harder than this," she went on. "Something quite commonplace and comfortable. I must go back to Claybrooke to-morrow, and try to please and comfort those whom, in my selfish pride, I thrust aside and scorned.—I have made a great failure.—Now I shall be content with very simple duties.—I shall be humble in future

I think, and quite willing to take the lowest room. There are better things in life than happiness perhaps.—But it is sad," she added, looking away, and speaking more to herself than to him, "it is all very sad. It is all over for me ;—and the long years stretch out so gray and level into the distance ;—and I shall be all alone ;—and I am so young."

The last few words moved Wharton strangely. She was very young ; and the mystery and tragedy of it all seemed to him infinite. As he looked at her in her piteous beauty and sorrow, Wharton read his own heart clear.—Friendship seemed to him a very pale and intangible good ; his philosophies took to themselves wings and flew away ; all his doubts and indecisions resolved themselves into one passionate desire. His face grew thin and eager, and a great light came into his eyes. He forgot everything else. He only knew that, amid warmth, and light, and the penetrating sweetness of flowers, he was standing alone, face to face, with the woman he loved.

Wharton threw back his head and took a long deep breath. It seemed to him he had never really lived till now.

Elizabeth was struck with the change in his appearance; it almost frightened her. Instinctively she moved a step back.

" Elizabeth, listen to me," he said, bending towards her; " listen—I love you. I know that I love you. Look, dearest, I know I am not worth very much. I have been a light-minded frivolous creature enough all my days. But I will love and honour you; I will serve you early and late; your lightest wish shall be my law. I will be your very slave. I believe I could make you very happy, Elizabeth— only love me, darling," he said, " love me."

The young man's eager face, the words of passionate tenderness and worship, were very wonderful coming to Elizabeth at this moment. She had sunk very low in her own estimation, all her pride was humbled in the dust—and now suddenly, unexpectedly, came this offer of love and protection.

"Ah!" she said, "how can I love you? I dare not love you after all the past."

"We will forget all the past," he answered. "We will both begin life anew from to-night. The future is ours—only love me, Elizabeth."

Do not despise poor Elizabeth if she hesitated. She had taken but a few steps along the rugged way of penitence and self-denial that leads up—as we trust,—at last, to the perfected glory and peace of heaven. Saints and martyrs have paused and turned pale at sight of that hard stony road winding up the bare hillside. What wonder if this delicate, weak, and erring woman should cast longing backward glances at the green pastures and still waters in the valley below? What

wonder if gentle companionship, if love,
and beauty, and common human joys,
should tempt her?—if more tender hopes
even than these—hopes which like every
true woman she had cherished, and which
it had been her lot to see wither and die
—should move her to give way? Tiny
baby-hands seemed for a moment to press
about her bosom, and sweet baby-lips to
meet her own in clinging kisses.

With eyes dim with strange half-happy
tears, with a smile dawning again on her
pale and weary face, she stood looking at
her waiting lover.

Wharton thought he read her answer.

"Elizabeth!" he said, in a tone of
triumphant joy, and stretched out both
his hands with an impetuous gesture to
take hers.

As he did so the wooden rosary slipped
from her yielding fingers and fell with a
hard dry rattle on to the floor.

Wharton and Elizabeth started apart.

In moments of vivid excitement and deep emotion a very small incident may change the course of feeling, and consequently of events. That time-honoured symbol of prayer, and penitence, and humility, with its roughly-carved image of the dying Saviour of mankind, seemed suddenly to interpose an invisible, but impenetrable barrier between the two lovers.

Elizabeth was the first to speak. Her voice sounded thin and far off, as though it came from a great distance.

"I cannot marry you," she said; "I belong to my dead husband."

"A living love is better than a dead love!" cried Wharton fiercely.

"The greatest love must die to gain that which it loves," she answered, pointing to the crucifix lying among the scattered flowers.

"Elizabeth," said Wharton desperately, "you dare not be so cruel. Through

my love for you I have found a new life.
Have you given me a soul merely to
damn it?"

Elizabeth covered her face with her
hands. The temptation to yield to his
pleading was almost irresistible. It is so
difficult in the face of that which is seen
o cling to that which, though unseen, is
yet eternal. But Elizabeth had, at last,
perceived that through the wilderness of
this life there stretches a "more excellent
way;" and she dared not wander from it
in search of mere temporal happiness.

When she spoke again she was quite
still and calm.

"You must go," she said. "God is
good; He will guide us both. I cannot
marry you."

The last appeal of the civilised man,
like the first appeal of the savage, is, after
all, to the senses. As a drowning man
clutches at straws, so Wharton clutched
at his last chance. He came close to

Elizabeth, and looked her full in the face.

"I will go," he said: "but first you must kiss me—only once, Elizabeth."

She flushed all rosy red: but she met his eyes steadily.

"You must go," she answered, "and I will not kiss you, even once."

Wharton turned away sick at heart.

His old, easy-going, pleasant life seemed shattered and broken, and at this moment he had little enough hope that a better life would rise from its ruins. The passion, which had so suddenly developed within him, left him bitter and unsatisfied. He was going through those dark and troubled waters which all the nobler natures among us must struggle through, at least once, if we are to learn anything real concerning our own hearts and the world around us. He knew that it was hopeless to try any more to move Elizabeth. He was weary of the battle and the anguish.

"Good-bye, Mrs. Lorimer," he said. " You have given me the greatest joys and the greatest sorrows of my life."

Elizabeth could not trust herself to answer. She merely gave him her hand. He took it and, bending down, kissed it lightly. Then he went slowly away.

Wharton looked back once. Elizabeth stood, a tall, glimmering, white figure among the fading narcissus flowers, with sad, wide-open, gray eyes, and a dull red stain upon her breast.

A few minutes later she had taken the little sketch of Robert Lorimer from its narrow resting-place in the writing-table drawer. Perhaps there is no purer joy in life, after all, than the joy of restitution.

CHAPTER XI.

"The true order of approaching to the things of love is
to use the beauties of earth as steps along which to
mount upward to that other beauty, rising from the
love of one to the love of two, and from the love of
two to the love of all fair forms, and from the love of
fair forms to fair deeds, and from fair deeds to fair
thoughts, till from fair thoughts he reaches on to the
thought of the Uncreated loveliness, and at last knows
what true beauty is."

THE next morning Elizabeth and Martha
—the latter not a little bewildered by
her mistress's sudden change of plans—
travelled down to Slowby. It was a bright
mild spring-day. The wind blew softly
across the broad pastures, and the elm-
buds blushed red in the sunshine. Here
and there, the blossom of the blackthorn
still lay like a thin snow-wreath upon the
hedges. The larch-trees had put on their

dainty garment of green. In the spinnies the ground was starred with white anemone flowers, and the first primroses tempted the village children to wander far afield, between morning and afternoon school ; while the cloud-shadows flitted lightly across the face of the country, and the lines of the distant woods looked infinitely far and still in the clear atmosphere.

Elizabeth had telegraphed to Mr. Mainwaring early in the morning. She knew that telegrams were regarded with small favour at the Rectory, as one of the many superfluous and agitating develop-ments of modern civilisation. Respect-able and well-regulated persons should always know their plans beforehand ; and only in cases of the direst necessity should they have recourse to this urgent, and rather undignified, method of communicat-ing with their families. Mrs. Mainwaring held that it is always vulgar to appear in a hurry. But Elizabeth could not stop just

now to consider the possible effects of
her telegram upon her aunt's mind. She
wanted desperately to get away from
London at once. She dared not run the
risk of meeting Wharton again, and she
dreaded the thought of a catechism from
Fanny Lorimer concerning her sudden
change of plans.

She had grasped the idea of penance
with all the energy of her ardent nature,
and while the emotion was still strong
within her she felt a feverish desire to
break utterly with her past life, and to
make her peace with her aunt and uncle.
She was possessed with the passionate
longing for entire self-surrender that has
made torture and death an actual joy
to thousands. She was in love with a
new and exquisite ideal which had presented itself to her; and she could neither
pause nor rest till she had made the offering of herself complete. This is a somewhat perilous state of feeling. It can

meet the rack or the stake with a splendid courage : but it has a tendency to grow rather thin, and tired, and acid, when the crown of glory is not quickly awarded, and when it is tested by the steady strain of every day.

Claybrooke Rectory has always struck me as a very composed place. It does not look as if its inhabitants would ever be the victims of overmuch spiritual exaltation. There is a suggestion of kindly and secure well-being about its warm sober - colouring, solid masonry, quaint gables and windows, and about its well-kept lawns and gardens, which is certainly soothing and reassuring. Some places incline one instinctively to take comfortable views of this world and the next ; and dispose one to wonder whether, after all, there is not a great deal to be said on the side of the Universalists.

Rufus, the old brown retriever, roused himself from a nap on the broad doorstep as Elizabeth got out of the carriage. He wagged his tail slowly, and smiled a lazy welcome to his former playmate : but he did not feel it necessary to express any more active joy at her return. Rufus had reached the time of life—common to dogs and men alike—when warmth is the greatest good, and cold the greatest evil, of existence ; when no event is very surprising, and the mind is willing to acquiesce in any state of things short of actual physical distress.

The softly radiant spring-day, the stately calm of the house, and the old dog sleeping his easy life away on the sunny doorstep, formed a strange and pathetic contrast to the rapid movements, and worn eager face of the beautiful young woman, who passed hastily indoors.

The Rector was out, and Mrs. Mainwaring was upstairs. They had not expected Mrs. Lorimer till the afternoon train — so said Bunton when he met

Elizabeth in the hall. He was slightly put about, being unaccustomed to sudden arrivals, and to that reversal of preconceived ideas which they produce.

Elizabeth went swiftly upstairs, along the dark wainscoted landing, and opened the sitting-room door.

The scene within was very calm and sweetly cheerful. The room, with its white panelled walls and light curtains, seemed full of sunshine. One of the windows stood open, and a soft breeze—bearing delicate scents of the fresh-turned earth, of the springing grass and opening leaves, —came in at it, and gently stirred the lappets of Mrs. Mainwaring's white lace cap, as she sat quietly knitting by the fire.

There was something in this peaceful little picture which affected Elizabeth strongly. The imperative, almost hard, expression died out of her face, and gave place to a wistful tenderness.

Mrs. Mainwaring looked up as the door

opened. Her forehead contracted slightly, and a pink flush came into her cheeks.

Elizabeth did not give her time either to rise or speak, but walked quickly across the room and knelt down on the hearth-rug before her.

"Aunt Susan," she said, and her voice took the tones of entreaty, while her eyes filled with tears, " I have been greatly to blame. I left you two years ago in the foolish pride of my heart : but I have been punished. Since then I have learnt a hard lesson. I have come back to ask your forgiveness. I will be gentle and patient, I will try my utmost to please you,—I will be like your own daughter, —if you will only forgive me and let me come home."

Elizabeth's little speech ended in a sob.

All the hungry unsatisfied mother-love in Mrs. Mainwaring awoke and yearned towards the fair woman before her. She stayed neither to ask questions nor read a moral. She merely put out both her hands and drew the sweet weary head down to rest upon her bosom.

"My poor child," she said softly, "you are very welcome home. Perhaps we both have made mistakes in the past, but we will forget them. It must only be a question of love, not of forgiveness, between you and me."

"Ah!" said Elizabeth, with a restful sigh—like that of a little child, which, having lost its way and wandered far and wide, finds itself safe, at last, in its mother's arms again—"Ah! you do forgive me, dear Aunt Susie? I know I did wrong: but I am sorry, and I am so very very tired."

Mrs. Mainwaring stooped and kissed her forehead.

"Well then, darling, rest," she said.

It must be owned that the middles of things are always rather trying. Begin-

nings are full of hope and promise. We
have been disappointed many times before,
certainly : but, a fig for past disappointments!—this time all will surely go straight.
Endings, though too often touched with
dissatisfaction and regret, still have a promise of coming repose or change about
them, which is generally more or less
grateful. The morning and the evening
are romantic, and one can think of a hundred and one pretty things to say concerning them : but it argues a very strenuous
and active state of mind,—or a certain
quality of wholesome dulness in one's com-
position,—if one can honestly sing the
praises of the middle-day.

The morning of poor Elizabeth's repentance was strong and fresh. Nothing
seemed too hard for her to dare, too
difficult for her to undertake. But in
healthy natures spiritual development is
almost always gradual. There may be a
moment of sudden awakening, when the

head and heart alike are convinced of
error ; and the recognition of that error
may produce a lasting effect on the
character. But resignation and self-renunciation cannot be perfected in a
moment. The perfecting of them is a
long and arduous process, during which
the poor soul, driven forth from its old
dwelling-place and fainting in the arid
wilderness, loses faith and courage at
times, and cries out with hungry longing
after the flesh-pots of its forsaken Egypt.

For a while the passionate feeling, born
of love to her dead husband and bitter
sorrow for her past wilfulness, supported
Elizabeth. The breaking wave carried
her far up the shore. But later, when the
first intensity of her feeling had subsided,
when mere emotion was required to crys-
tallise into steady habit, there came a
season of trial and danger,—a time of
what old devotional writers call " spiritual
dryness,"—in which she was tempted to

think her faults of little importance, and her repentance exaggerated; and when the fair and stately ideal of the religious life grew pale and misty to her tired eyes.

She struggled bravely, for she had a noble spirit. She never quite lost her hold of the deep truths which she had grasped: but at times she was sad and restless, and the way seemed very long, and the burden very heavy. Victory is, too often, a melancholy business, after all. The battle may gallantly be fought and fairly won; yet afterwards there must be days of anguish for the wounded, and of mourning for the dead, and of heavy sorrow at sight of the trampled fields and ruined homesteads.

The promise is to those that "endure." And notwithstanding depression and self-distrust Elizabeth Lorimer did endure; and in time she was rewarded. She began, at last, to know the inward peace which springs from the absence of personal

desire, and the serenity which grows out
of true self-renunciation.   In proportion
as she ceased to love her own narrow life,
she began to find a richer and wider life
in sympathy with those around her.   Acts
of charity and of self-denial, which before
had appeared to her only as tiresome
obligations to her fellow-creatures, now
became in a way sacramental,—symbols
of faithful obedience to God and loving
brotherhood with man.   Elizabeth was
learning, slowly and painfully, to exchange
the love of her own fancies for the love of
certain Eternal Verities,—doubted, scorned,
pushed angrily aside by generation after
generation ; yet always abiding, patiently
reasserting themselves, ever ready to be
revealed in infinite sweetness and consolation to the broken and contrite heart.

It may seem slightly eccentric to
describe the moral and spiritual experiences of a modern young lady,— who
ministers to one's material wants at five

o'clock tea, and does not disdain to make herself agreeable in ordinary society—in terms which are usually reserved for the delineation of a mediæval saint. But though the outward conditions and circumstances change, the vital processes of the human mind are very much alike in the first century and in the nineteenth. Given a certain type of character, its mental history will be nearly the same in every age.

It is certain, any way, that those who, like myself, had the privilege of seeing something of Mrs. Lorimer during the months that followed her return to Claybrooke, perceived a very distinct change in her.

Personally I must own to having been a good deal occupied about Mrs. Lorimer at this period; though I am afraid she was utterly indifferent to my sentimental condition,—if, indeed, she was even aware of its existence. She had lost some of her queenliness, some of the rich bloom of her early beauty : but, to me at least, she had never appeared more captivating.   There was something in her face which reminded one of the still purity of the open sky, when the heavy storm-clouds are all rolled away and the evening light spreads itself, with a tender radiance, over the resting land.   There was a sweet reasonableness, and a certain gracious humility, about her. She was gentle and friendly, scorning no little deeds of kindly service to those around her.

The people of Claybrooke, who heretofore had regarded her merely as Mr. Mainwaring's heiress—as a young lady whose position and personal charms created a rather dramatic atmosphere about her, the observation of which might afford some innocent excitement to humbler individuals—now began to reckon upon her sure help and quick sympathy in all their troubles.   Instinctively men of her

own class treated her with the delicate
courtesy and reverence which it should
be the right of every woman to receive at
the hands of every man : but which it is
really a little difficult to accord to the
alarmingly vigorous, lawn-tennis-playing
damsels of the present day.

I do not doubt but that Mrs. Lorimer
had sad hours, lonely hours, hours of disappointment and regret, that she was
annoyed, and disheartened, and distressed,
sometimes like the rest of us. In compar-
ing her to the saints, I am very far from
wishing to imply that she was faultless ;—
indeed, I am disposed to think, that if the
saints themselves had not made a good
many mistakes, at times, while they were
here on earth, there would be little enough
temptation to ask their prayers now that
they are safe in heaven. I would only say
that I believe Elizabeth,—like her noble
Thuringian namesake,—having once perceived the deepest meaning of this life,

and having seen that "more excellent way," walked along it steadfastly, with a fine and simple courage, while the light about her shone clearer and clearer towards the perfect day.

If such things do not and cannot happen, if lives cannot be so lived, then indeed we are most miserable; for the fairest ideal of human attainment that has ever been vouchsafed to poor struggling men and women is, after all, but a delusion and a lie.

CHAPTER XII.

"Fear no more the heat o' the sun
  Nor the furious winter's rages ;
Thou thy worldly task hast done,
  Home art gone and ta'en thy wages :
Golden lads and girls all must,
  As chimney sweepers, come to dust."

THAT summer was very wet,—it rained
in June, and in July, and right on into
September. At Claybrooke the stream,
from which the parish takes its name,
overflowed, and the low-lying lands in the
valley were more or less under water for
months. There was a good deal of illness
and fever about. The potatoes rotted in
the ground, and the wheat grew in the
shocks before it could be gathered in. In
our heavy clay country a wet summer is a
very nasty business.

Meanwhile, Mrs. Frank Lorimer, notwithstanding Elizabeth's defection, held
stoutly to the plan of spending the summer
in Switzerland. Frank protested on the score
of expense and of the difficulty of taking
two small children such a long journey :
but, his wife having made up her mind, he,
as usual, ended by giving way. So by
the middle of August, the Frank Lorimers
found themselves established in one of
those charming little towns that fringe
the northern shores of the Lake of Geneva,
with their rows of white houses.

Wharton had joined the party—he
would really have been at a loss to state
exactly why. His feelings towards Mrs.
Frank were certainly not of an ardently
affectionate nature : but he liked her husband. Too he felt, deep down in his heart,
a sort of morose satisfaction in being with
Elizabeth Lorimer's relations, and in pick-
ing up stray bits of information about her
from time to time.

A change had come over Wharton in the last few months. He was more silent and preoccupied, less cheery and expansive, and he looked a good deal older. He had been drawing hard lately; and intelligent critics thought they perceived a new quality in his work. It was less delicately pretty, but stronger, and with more meaning and directness of intention about it. One or two people were good enough to prophesy concerning him that he would still make his mark. When some acquaintance asked him, one day, how he had come suddenly to make such a distinct advance and improvement, he shrugged his shoulders and answered, with a laugh—

"Oh, you know, this child too has been in hell!"

The Frank Lorimers were very prosperous people. Things as a rule went easily and pleasantly with them : but just at this period they seemed to get a run of bad luck.

The weather was almost as wet in "the beautiful Pays de Vaud" as at home in England. A daily thunder-storm came to be reckoned as regularly included in the bill of fare. The children were poorly and fretful; and, as a very crown of trouble, Frank managed, while doing a little rudimentary mountaineering, to slip on some loose rock and sprain his ankle. It caused him acute pain at the time, and obliged him to spend the best part of a month on the sofa, swearing mildly at foreign countries in general and at mountainous countries in particular; and declaring that he, for his part, should spend his next holiday at Margate, dine at one o'clock, and have shrimps every evening for tea, let Fanny say what she liked.

On a certain Monday afternoon, while the daily thunder-storm was cannonading backwards and forwards among the hills, the Lorimers were trying to amuse themselves, as well as they could, in their little *salon*. It was a not very luxurious apartment—possessed of solid furniture and a superfluity of faded, red, Utrecht velvet—on the second floor of the hotel : but it had the charm of possessing, also, two great French windows opening on to a balcony, which commanded a splendid view—when anything was to be seen.

Frank was lying on the sofa, grumbling gently. To come abroad at considerable expense, and then be laid up in this way, was enough to turn even his amiable nature a little sour. Mrs. Frank was struggling to take a vital interest in a Tauchnitz novel—concerning which she had a horrid suspicion that the third volume was lost,—and, alternately, listening to hear if the baby " sounded happy " with his nurse in the next room, and admonishing Nini, who, bored and irritable at being kept so much indoors, seemed to be meditating unspeakable atrocities upon the now-no-longer-new " dollie with the pink hat." Fred Wharton stood lazily at the open window, with his hands in his pockets and his back to the company, watching the progress of the storm. He had developed rather a habit of standing moodily doing nothing but stare out of the window just lately.

The prospect was not a cheering one. Across the lake, the mountains of Savoy and of the Valais were sulking behind heavy streaming masses of white mist. Down towards Geneva there was a lurid light in the sky, and the swiftly-moving copper-coloured clouds were twisted and contorted into a thousand weird fantastic shapes. The broad lake, itself, was a murky blue, with long zigzagged flaws of livid gray, where the sudden gusts of wind swept across the angry surface of the water. In the foreground, Wharton could see the waves dashing themselves fitfully against the stone wall on the other

side of the roadway ; while great drops of
rain splashed and pattered on the broad
leaves of the pollarded plane-trees in the
garden just below.   It was not an encouraging outlook, certainly : but perhaps
Wharton was none the less in sympathy
with it on that account.

There was a knock at the door of the
salon.

"*Entrez !* " cried Mrs. Frank over her
shoulder.

Then, turning to the little girl on the
floor by her side, she said :—

" Nini, my dear child, do have some sort
of compassion on that unfortunate doll.
You'll break its head right off, you know,
if you bang it down on the floor in that
way."

Nini looked up, with a very mutinous
little face, at her mother, and banged the
doll's head down again on the bare *parquet*
floor.

" I hate this dollie," she said petulantly,

she's so old. I want to go out into the garden and play."

Wharton turned round as the door opened. It was only a hurried and slightly distracted *garçon* with a packet of English letters.

" None for you, Fred," said Frank Lorimer, as he examined them slowly, before proceeding to open them.

Wharton turned back to the window again.

" Good gracious ! " cried Frank all of a sudden.

" Why, what's the matter ? " asked his wife. Almost any event would have been a relief to her this afternoon, she felt so unutterably bored.

" Elizabeth's ill, down at Claybrooke," said Frank slowly, running his eyes over the pages of the letter. " Old Mr. Mainwaring writes. They want me to go there at once."

Wharton set his teeth rather hard, as he

watched the flaws of wind chasing each
other across the sullen face of the lake.
He remembered Elizabeth Lorimer as he
had seen her last, standing, pale and
patient, in her white dress among the
scattered flowers. He had told her once
that presentiments were silly things : but
he thought, with a sickening feeling of
dread, of the dull red stain upon her
bosom.

"Fanny, come here!" cried Frank
sharply. "Look here, this letter's a good
week old. It was sent to London, and
evidently it wasn't forwarded for several
days."

Fanny Lorimer moved quickly across
the room, and kneeling down by her
husband's side began reading the letter.

"Anything may have happened by
this time," Frank said. "What on earth
am I to do?"

"Oh! I'm afraid she is really very ill.
I am afraid it is serious," said Fanny

Lorimer in accents of genuine alarm and distress. "I tell you what, Frank," she went on, getting up and standing by him with a pretty air of determination, "I must go off to her at once, this very evening."

"Indeed you'll do nothing of the kind," he answered shortly.

Like a good many other people, Frank had a habit of getting remarkably cross when he was frightened.

"It's quite bad enough to have Elizabeth catching a nasty fever, going and poking about in beastly cottages, without your rushing off to look after her and catching it too. And I've not the least intention of being left here, tied by the leg, with a grumbling nurse and a couple of naughty children on my hands, I can tell you."

"I'm sure the children are not particularly naughty," answered Fanny Lorimer, who in the very article of death would have bustled up to defend the reputation of the two babies.

"I don't know what on earth to do, though," said Frank despairingly.

Fred Wharton had turned round and was standing with his back to the window. He had formed a definite plan in his own mind, but he wanted to propose it quietly ; and make it appear the most natural and obvious course in the world, both to himself and to his companions.

He sauntered slowly up to the sofa.

"One thing is certain, any way, Frank," he said quietly, "you can't travel."

"I know," answered the other man dismally. "I hope I'm not a great coward, you know, but I really don't think I could."

"And Mrs. Lorimer can't be spared," added Wharton ; "that's clear."

Fanny Lorimer glanced up at him quickly. She held her own opinion as to what had made Elizabeth suddenly retire to Claybrooke, and Wharton become so silent and moody. Even at this moment of real trouble on her part,—for she was very fond of Elizabeth,—she could not resist trying to gain some hints regarding past events from his manner and expression.

Wharton looked at her steadily ; there was something rather hard and unpleasant in his face, which made Fanny Lorimer drop her eyes quickly on to the open letter again.

" If you write," he continued ; " it will be at least five or six days before you get any answer. If you telegraph you can't explain all your reasons for not coming, and they may not unreasonably think you rather indifferent and unsympathetic." He paused a minute. " I really think you'd better let me go," he added. " I can catch the evening train through to Paris. You know I could go right on down to Clay-brooke and telegraph you the real state of the case."

" You really are the best fellow in the

world, Fred," said Frank Lorimer, his face clearing up considerably. " I shall be everlastingly grateful to you."

Whatever Fanny Lorimer's feelings may have been, she hid them under a charming smile of relief and gratitude, and made no objection.

All that night, and through the next day, as he travelled north—in noisy trains, on the steamboat, and at crowded stations —Fred Wharton was haunted with a vision of Elizabeth Lorimer, in her white gown, with the rough rosary in her hands, and the red stain upon her bosom. He had a lurking terror of what he might hear at the end of his journey; and, at the same time, a wild hope that somehow he should see her and plead with her, and that, this time, she would yield to his pleading. He knew, only too well, that he loved her desperately, and he hoped on still against hope.

Tired, haggard, and dirty, he arrived at

quiet little Slowby early on the second day after leaving Switzerland. Hiring a cab, he drove straight over to Claybrooke by the broad, high-lying, main road. The rain was falling in a steady downpour, and all the distant country was blotted out with impenetrable mist. When at length he got to Claybrooke, Wharton left his cab in the village street and walked alone up to the house.

He could almost have cried out loud in the intensity of his suspense, as he stood waiting on the doorstep. When the butler opened the door Wharton glanced at him sharply. There was something odd, he fancied, about the man's bearing and manner.

"Tell me," he said hoarsely, "how is Mrs. Lorimer?"

Bunton stared at him for a moment; he seemed hardly to know how to answer.

"Don't you know, sir?" he asked slowly "Haven't you heard?"

"No, no," cried Wharton impatiently.
"Why, if I had heard, I shouldn't come
here now to ask."

Bunton waited a minute or two before
speaking. He looked back into the
great sombre hall behind him, and out
across the carriage-sweep, as though he
hoped that from somewhere somebody
would come and help him.

At last he said simply—

"The funeral was yesterday at noon, sir."

Wharton threw up his two hands and
staggered back against the doorpost.

"Good God," he said under his breath,
"she is dead."

It was all over. He would never plead
with her and she would never yield to his
entreaties. The great black curtain had
been drawn between them for ever, and
he would never see her lovely face in this
world again.

Far away inside the house a door
banged. Then Wharton heard footsteps

in the garden, and a tall man with straight clear-cut features and deep-set, keen, gray eyes, in a long white mackintosh, gaiters and shooting boots, came slowly round the corner of the rambling old house. Wharton knew directly that it must be Mr. Mainwaring, from the subtle likeness he bore to Elizabeth.

But Mr. Mainwaring had aged very much since the afternoon that he rode home, in the chill and dusk, from his long day's hunting, seven months before. There were deep lines about his mouth, as though he had suffered some heavy sorrow which had eaten into his very heart. He walked with his head a little forward and his shoulders somewhat bent. Leaping about him were the two fox-terriers Billy and Boxer. Evidently they had only just been let out, and were in a state of frantic joy.

"Get down, dogs, get down!" said Mr. Mainwaring testily. "Can't you be quiet

for once in your lives, you senseless
brutes?"

Looking up, he caught sight of Wharton
in the doorway.

"Who's that?" he said sharply. "What's
the matter? Is the man ill?"

At any other time Wharton would probably have resented this somewhat un-
courteous address pretty strongly: but
now he was too broken down to care to
stand upon his dignity.

"I have just heard some news from your
servant here," he said, "which has shocked
me inexpressibly."

Mr. Mainwaring paused and looked
at him. Wharton's personal appearance
was, naturally, not improved by his
long and hurried journey: but Mr. Mainwaring saw that, whatever his business
might be, he was undoubtedly a gentleman.

"I come from Frank Lorimer," said
Wharton.

" He ought to have come himself, long ago," answered Mr. Mainwaring harshly.

" They are abroad," said Wharton. " Your letter only reached them the day before yesterday. Lorimer has had an accident ; he is laid up, and it was impossible for him to travel.—I knew Mrs. Lorimer very well," he added, looking Mr. Mainwaring full in the face. " I offered to come here and telegraph the latest news to them, but——"

Wharton's voice grew husky ; he could not manage to say any more.

Mr. Mainwaring turned away, and gazed down the carriage-drive, through the dull rain and mist.

" You are too late, sir," he said.

" I know it," Wharton answered, quietly enough : but he felt that Mr. Mainwaring's words cut right into his very heart.

All along he knew he had been just that :—" too late." It made him nearly mad to think it was possible—nay, even

probable,— that everything would have
ended so differently, but for his own
selfish and cowardly indecision ;—if he
had spoken, as he had been greatly
tempted to, when he met Elizabeth in
the windy twilight, that evening on the
Embankment. His misfortune, he feared,
was pretty much of his own making. He
had no one to blame for it, after all,
except himself ; and that reflection added
just the bitterest drop to the cup of his
sorrow. A sort of blind rage took possession of him at the thought of all he had
lost. He turned suddenly and fiercely
upon Mr. Mainwaring, regardless of the
strangeness of their relative position.

" But how did it happen?" he demanded.
" Why was she ill ? What—what have
you all been doing ?"

The two men were still standing on the
broad doorstep. Mr. Mainwaring had,
so far, made no proposal to Wharton to
come indoors. Mr. Mainwaring was not in

the habit of analysing his own sensations very acutely : but he was sensible that there was a certain dreary harmony between his present state of mind and the dull soaking day. And then, too, he felt unwilling to take this stranger into the house, still hushed and, in a way, sanctified by the recent presence of death. Mr. Mainwaring found this interview anything but pleasant. He desired to cut it as short as possible, and he thought it would be easier to do so standing out there in the wet. When Wharton's urgent reproachful questions sounded in his ears, he turned to the young man swiftly and proudly. It seemed to him almost insolent, and he felt disposed to make a harsh rejoinder and cut the interview very short indeed : but there was something in the expression of Wharton's face that arrested his attention.

Mr. Mainwaring looked at him keenly for a minute or two, while his grisled eyebrows contracted, and a straight line cut itself, deep and sharp, into his forehead. At last he answered quite calmly—

"You tell me you knew my niece well," he said:—"very well then, you must know that she was not easy to turn from any purpose she took in hand. She was a noble woman; she was stubborn and determined in carrying through that which she believed to be right."

Wharton bowed. He felt that he had spoken intemperately, and that his companion's courtesy exceeded his deserts.

"My niece," Mr. Mainwaring went on slowly and doggedly, as though compelling himself to speak—"was not one of those dainty persons who are content to let their religion walk in silver slippers; who plume themselves on being very much distressed by suffering, while they do nothing practical to lessen it. My niece Elizabeth's virtues were not of the sentimental and hysterical order."

Mr. Mainwaring paused a moment, looked away, and then spoke again, with the same quiet determination.

"We've had a very bad season," he said. "There has been fever here, off and on, all the summer, from the floods and the wet. My wife and I wanted her— wanted Elizabeth—to go away, and get out of it all. But she wouldn't. She wouldn't leave us and the people. She chose to stay and work.—She comforted those who were in trouble and nursed the sick with her own hands. It was not a very pleasant office," he added : "but she went through with it all ; and behaved like the gracious, and fearless, and godly woman that she was."

Mr. Mainwaring drew himself up, and looked at Wharton with a somewhat bitter smile.

"Verily she had her reward," he went on. "She pulled a lot of cases through by sheer pluck and patience. She was loved and honoured by all.   And then, one day, she got a cold, or a chill, or something, and she sickened herself, and——"

Mr. Mainwaring's voice broke suddenly.

" Now you know all I have to tell you," he added, after a minute or two.

Wharton had nothing to answer.   He stood looking on the ground, lost in a maze of strange and painful reflections. With Elizabeth, he felt, it must be well, for she had fulfilled her highest ideal ; —and that, not aided by romantic and sympathetic surroundings, in an atmosphere charged with the spirit of sacred devotion: but hardly, in the plain commonplace life of a dull, little, Midlandshire village.   A clay soil, a wet summer, a bad harvest, very ordinary, stolid, labouring men and women ill with fever, a certain determination to go her own way—call it foolhardy or heroic, as you please—with a background of solid comfort, secure prosperity, calm respectability ;—these were the curiously unexciting conditions of Elizabeth Lorimer's martyrdom.

Thinking of the sweetness of her youthful grace and beauty, and of her fate, Wharton was filled with awe and bewilderment. For a time his own personal sorrow was swallowed up in wonder. He could not understand it.

Suddenly he turned again to Mr. Mainwaring, who had been watching him in silence.

"What does it all mean?" he asked, with a fierce desperation.

Mr. Mainwaring gave himself a sort of shake.

"Ah, young man, who shall answer you that question?" he said. "Not I; nor men far wiser than I am."

Mr. Mainwaring was not in the habit of jumping at conclusions; he was too stately a person for that: but as he stood watching his companion he had arrived at a pretty distinct perception of the situation.   He came a step nearer, and laid his hand quietly on Fred Wharton's shoulder.

" You loved my niece," he said in a low voice.

" Ah God ! how I did love her !" cried Wharton passionately, stung into vivid consciousness of the magnitude of his own misery and desolation again.

" Poor boy ! poor boy !" said Mr. Mainwaring gently.

His face was full of compassion ; yet he could have found it in his heart to envy the younger man the wild energy of his sorrow.

Mr. Mainwaring's grief was of a very different complexion.   It did not strive or cry, it was patient and dry-eyed : but he knew that it would rise early and late take rest ; that it would make him eat the bread of affliction and drink the waters of bitterness, through all the coming days and years, till his body should be laid, there, in the quiet country churchyard ; and till his soul too should have found its rest, at last, in the blessed calm of " the land that is very far off."

" In losing her I have lost everything," said Wharton in a despairing voice.

" No, no," answered Mr. Mainwaring, quickly and almost sternly ; " you have not lost everything.   Your faith is left you as a Christian ; your honour is left you as a gentleman ; your work of some sort is left you too, I suppose ;—or if you have no work it is easy enough to find some,—there's plenty waiting to be done on every side.   You're very hard hit just now : but remember you're not alone. Sad things happen every day ; worse things than have happened to you.   Yes, worse things even than death, and than knowing you will never hold the woman you love in your arms."   He paused, and then went on kindly—" After all, you know, time is on your side.   You are young yet, and all the best of your life

may still be before you. A man at your
age gets over a blow like this with a few
ugly scars ; while a man of my age just
bleeds quietly to death."

Mr. Mainwaring smiled a little as he
said the last few words, and stuck out his
under lip.

Wharton stood fairly awed before the
strength which could smile thus stoic-
ally at its own suffering. It seemed to
pull him together somehow, and give him
courage to face the world again.

" Thank you," he said simply.

The wind—which had risen considerably
in the course of the last hour, and promised
to clear the sky of clouds by mid-day,—
rushed through the swaying tree - tops,
dashed the drops from the glistening
laurels on either side the carriage-drive,
and cried and called plaintively round the
gables of the old sandstone house. There
was a little space of silence, between the
two men who, each in his own way, had

so truly loved one woman. Then Mr. Mainwaring raised his hat, and standing there, uncovered, in the driving rain, said very calmly and reverently—

"Ah, my dear little Lizzie! God rest her sweet soul!"

THE END.